Vic Scott was born in Scotland. He completed two years of National Service in Malaya, North Borneo, and Singapore in a special unit. He joined an English county police force before retiring in 1985 as an Inspector. He has lived in Spain and took up residence in Thailand in 2005 where he now lives with his wife.

Vic Scott

CHAMELEON

AUSTIN MACAULEY PUBLISHERS™

LONDON • CAMBRIDGE • NEW YORK • SHARJAH

A CIP catalogue record for this title is available from the British Library.

ISBN 9781035822003 (Paperback)
ISBN 9781035822010 (ePub e-book)

www.austinmacauley.com

First Published 2024
Austin Macauley Publishers Ltd®
1 Canada Square
Canary Wharf
London
E14 5AA

Lomond Hills, Fife, Scotland

It was a bright morning in October, the sun had risen but the air had a sharp cold edge. The man left his home, an old hunting lodge which had been modernised, converted into a two-bedroom house with a large lounge, study, kitchen, toilet/shower room on the ground floor. It was comfortably furnished, a mixture of old and new styles. The kitchen was ultra-modern, large enough for a table and four chairs, a large refrigerator and a chest deep freeze, a gas stove plus an electric two ring cooking appliance. A central heating appliance was also installed.

In the large lounge, there was a Chesterfield settee, two armchairs, a coffee table. A 50-inch flat screen television together with a DVD player was on a long cabinet which housed a large collection of DVDs. A glass-fronted drinks cabinet was against one wall. Bookcases were arrayed along the rest of the wall space. They contained a diverse number of books, biographies, travel books, novels, large-scale map books.

One unusual feature was the existence of a floor safe, hidden under a wood panel, wood covered the floor, on top of which were several rugs. Inside the safe were several passports, different names, several countries. Wads of different currencies, U.S. dollars, euros and sterling mainly. A Glock handgun with a 17-shot magazine was inserted in the weapon ready for instant use.

The property had been purchased some time before the man started to reside there some nine months ago. There was a separate garage which contained a 4 x 4 Toyota, four-seat pickup truck, a recent model plus a Yamaha 250 c.c. motorcycle. The garage was locked by means of a metal bar and large padlock.

The lodge was sited about 600 yards from the Falkland Strathmiglo road in a forest of evergreen trees, it was not visible from the road, a single rough track led to it, about 400 yards from the house there was a barred wooden gate, secured by a chain and padlock which denied further access. Marlowe.

The man who called himself Sam Marlowe at the present time was mid-40s, 5 feet 10 inches tall, weight was 12 stone plus, not one spare ounce on him, extremely fit, clean shaven, weathered complexion, pale grey/blue eyes, crow's feet at the corners, facially nothing unusual, a plain countenance. Brown hair, a mite long but neat, he could pass unnoticed anywhere. He was an expert in several martial arts, possessing black belts in high grades. He was proficient. In outdoor activities, well above average in all his pursuits, skiing, rock climbing, canoeing, skydiving. In his youth, he had played several sports representing his school and college.

He was dressed for a long hike, woollen shirt, climbing breeches, long wool stockings, light suede hiking boots with Vibram soles, woollen ski hat, in his rucksack was a duvet jacket, spare stockings, a flask of coffee, another smaller flask containing hot vegetable soup, a plastic box of cheese and pickle sandwiches, two Mars' bars, a tube of mint sweets. He also carried a compass, a camera and around his neck hung powerful binoculars. He ambled through the trees ascending gradually. He loved walking in mountainous regions; he liked the solitude, the glimpses of wildlife, birds and animals. For personal reasons, he was virtually a recluse. He shunned company though in the past he had several relationships with the fairer sex. He was not celibate, when he felt the desire for intimate company, he would drive to Edinburgh, visit a nightclub and end up spending the night in a first-class hotel with willing, attractive feminine company. Because of his history, long-term relationships were not practical or wise. He did in fact have a two-year relationship which ended acrimoniously; he had regretted ending the relationship ever since.

As he climbed, he came out of the forest halfway up the slopes midway between the two hills. He saw a red squirrel, a fox lurking in the undergrowth, several birds. He felt content but was always aware of the surroundings and was alert constantly. He made his way to the West Lomond, there were several cliffs on the north side, he found a good spot and viewed the area, two rock climbers were scaling what looked like a hard route. He had refreshments and stayed there for nearly an hour. He continued to the summit, stayed there for some time. It was after 1 p.m. when he started his return hike. He was well above the tree line when he paused and scanned the area using his binoculars, paying particular attention to the area surrounding his lodge.

Between the lodge and the main road, he glimpsed something glinting in the sunshine; he focused on this, it was beyond the secured gate and near the drive just to the side in the trees. He spent time studying the object that dazzled in the sunlight and concluded that a vehicle was parked there. He cursed inwardly. He focused on the ground surrounding the lodge; he saw one man to the left about 100 yards from the lodge leaning against a tree. The man was smoking a cigarette, he was armed with a handgun, tucked in his waistband. "Bloody ferret," he murmured. "Now where is 'the Stoat'?"

He focused to the right and saw what he was looking for slightly closer to the lodge but further out, the man called 'the Stoat' was prone on the ground, looking towards the lodge, he was holding a handgun, a revolver. Their boss, the Huntmaster, would be inside the lodge waiting for the man to be delivered, unwillingly, to him by his two bodyguards.

An ice-cold fury enveloped the man, his privacy had been invaded and that he had been traced after a lengthy period of time. He had always been aware that it was a distinct possibility and he was not complacent but the fact that moment was now, dismayed him. His peaceful existence was now threatened. He began to stalk, aiming for the Ferret first, the man was a superb woodsman; he blended with nature, silent as a phantom, he moved from tree to tree, he picked up a thick piece of a branch, about four feet in length. He was about 15 feet away when he heard a conversation between the two watchers, they were using cell phones. The Ferret said, "Any sight of him?"

The reply was "No, I reckon he ain't here, this is a fucking waste of time."

"We have to stay until the boss says otherwise."

"Why the fuck he wants this wanker is beyond me."

"Because he's reckoned to be the best."

"Maybe once but he's over the fucking hill now."

The conversation ended; the man moved closer behind the tree the Ferret was leaning against. The makeshift club was swung in a wide arc, the blow struck the Ferret on the front of his head between the eyes, breaking skin, he slid down the tree trunk, out cold.

He was searched, a filthy handkerchief was found and stuffed in his mouth, plastic cuffs were discovered in his jacket pocket, they were used to bind the wrists and the ankles. The man took the handgun, a Smith and Wesson.38 revolver. He took possession of the cell phone and altered the setting to the silent mode. He dragged him behind the tree and laid him flat on the ground covered by the undergrowth.

Now, he started to encircle the other man's position, leaving at least 150 yards radius between them. Once he was behind the Stoat, he began to move towards him and came up behind and pressed the muzzle against the back of his head, "One move and you will have an extra orifice, nod if you understand, one word from you and you will have gained at least one extra hole, perhaps two." The Stoat nodded. "Place your weapon on the ground carefully with the barrel facing away, now arms fully stretched." He was searched, plastic cuffs, a packet of tissues, cell phone, a half tube of wine gums and coins plus his ID card in a wallet. His wrists were cuffed behind his back, his ankles too.

"I am going to ask you some questions, you whisper the answers, you raise your voice and you will end up toothless, nod if you understand." The Stoat nodded, fear showing in his eyes.

"The Boss is in the lodge, right?"

"Yeah."

"Who is with him?"

"Wolf."

"Why are you all here?"

"The Boss wants you for a special job. I don't know any more."

"I believe you, who in the hell is going to trust you two clowns? You have three options, I can gag you, I can knock you out or you can lie here and keep quiet, so what is it to be?"

"I'll be quiet."

"Okay, if I do hear you at all, I'll be back and it will not be pleasant for you."

"I give you my word."

Huntmaster

The man took a circuitous route which led him to the rear of the lodge where there was an entrance to the cellar. It was padlocked, he retrieved the key from under a stone and unlocked it. He removed the padlock and opened the two flaps of the entrance, not making a sound.

There were steps leading down to the cellar which he used as a storeroom and also had racks of bottles of wine. He closed the hatch and went to an interior flight of stairs which led to the kitchen. He stopped on the top stair and listened for several minutes at the door until he was sure there was no one in the kitchen. He opened the door, slowly and silently about, about a two-inch gap, he listened again; he could hear voices from beyond the kitchen, he entered the kitchen and went to the door which led into the lounge and listened, he recognised both voices.

Wolf: "Sir, if he suspects we are here, won't he clear off?"

Sir: "No, this is his home, he will be curious as to why we are here and how we managed to trace him."

Wolf: "He will be furious; he won't take on the job."

Sir: "He has no option; he won't like it but he will take on the assignment."

Wolf: "Why him? We have many operatives who are professional and who could do a good job."

Sir: "Perhaps but I have my doubts about our operatives. He is simply the best, the coolest in any situation. He is unique in many ways; he can operate at any level of society, he speaks more languages than anyone, all fluently and with regional dialects. He is the most ruthless, the deadliest man I have ever known or heard of. His record has never been matched and never will be. A master of disguise, his name Chameleon fits him."

Marlowe had heard enough, he was intrigued as to what the task was; he opened the door and entered the lounge. Wolf and Huntmaster were startled probably because of the handgun he was holding, they had risen to their feet, surprise written on their faces. "Sit down, I have a number of questions and I require answers, honest ones." Huntmaster said, "What have you done with Ferret and Stoat?"

"That is the first time I have ever heard any concern from you, they are alive, trussed up, Ferret will need some medical attention. Wolf, take a knife and release them and get Ferret to a clinic or hospital, Boss and I are going to have a chat."

Wolf looked at Huntmaster with a worried expression, "Do what Chameleon says, I'll be fine."

Marlowe said, "They are in the same positions, Ferret is under some branches, his injury is superficial, just looks bad, go." Wolf left.

Huntmaster was 60 years plus, a dapper man, 5 feet 8 inches tall, slim build, white cropped hair, trim moustache, a reddish complexion which suggested high blood pressure, a cultured voice, a product of Eton School and Oxford University. On leaving university, he served in the British

Security Service and was the director of a small elite unit specialising in Black Ops. An intelligent and ruthless man, during his career, he had accomplished many successes and very few failures.

Marlowe opened the discussion, "Why are you here? I walked away from the unit a year ago, I have no intention of returning and how the blazes did you find me?"

"Once in the firm, always in the firm, I allowed you to leave but I have known your movements since that day. You bought this place about nine months ago, you have been kept on ice until now, I have an assignment suited for your particular talents."

"Use someone else, I'm finished with your lot."

"You have no option, you have been with me over 15 years, I trained you, honed your skills, you never failed me, not once, you owe me."

"Get this, I am sick of carrying out assignments, sick of killing, I don't owe you anything, I have to live with my conscience, I want to live in peace, in solitude."

"To ease your conscience, every person you disposed of was evil, a necessity, they deserved their fate. I am not appealing to your vanity but I want you for this assignment simply because it is ideal for your talents. Do this for me, complete the task and I will endeavour to leave you in peace afterwards."

"Why don't I believe you?'

"I will do my best, I said I would try to leave you in peace, that is all I can promise you; will you listen to me?'

"I will listen but I am not making any commitment."

"Fair enough."

The Assignment

Huntmaster began, "What name are you using now?"

"Marlowe."

"Right, Marlowe, the target is Damian O'Reilly, have you heard the name?"

"I recall the name vaguely, wasn't he involved in a gold bullion robbery at Heathrow a couple of years ago?"

"Yes, he is also associated with other high value robberies, the Hatton Garden diamond heist last year, for instance. He was arrested on several occasions but the evidence was so flimsy that the police had to release him. Because of the police's continued interest and enquiries, he left the country, it is believed he visited central America, Australia and the Philippines, eventually he settled in Spain, the Costa Del Sol.

He lives in a luxury villa in the foothills outside Marbella; he bought the property a few years ago, renovated it, and added to it. He is a drugs baron, heroin, cocaine, cannabis, pills all being produced in Morocco. He has several high powered speed boats that do regular runs, their cargoes being unloaded at various sites on the Costa Del Sol. The drugs are then loaded into a variety of vehicles which are driven to private garages and warehouses.

There the drugs are hidden in vehicles carrying such items as fruit, vegetables, wine, olive oil, all destined for the UK. The vehicles are driven through Spain and France to the Channel tunnel; very few vehicles are checked, documents are always in order. Once in England, the drugs are distributed throughout the country. O'Reilly is the king, he plans, organises, owns the trucking businesses but he never goes near any of the locations, he stays aloof in his villa, directing everything through his henchman, Joseph Brown.

It is believed that Guardia Civil officers and local police officers are receiving monthly payments, off duty officers do stints as his bodyguards. The Home Office has requested his extradition and have sent the necessary documents. They have all been returned with letters attached stating that there is no real evidence contained in the documents and therefore could not be served on him. There was a footnote that warned that any attempt to remove O'Reilly would be unlawful and any person involved would be prosecuted in a Spanish court."

"So he is well protected, untouchable, why the effort to get him back into Britain, the evidence is still pretty thin?"

"They want his drugs business destroyed, the insurance companies want his hide and if possible recovery of the stolen proceeds, gold, diamonds etc. There is a reward for his capture plus a commission on any stolen items recovered. The reward could amount to well over a million pounds."

"Why me, surely you have capable operatives to carry out this task?"

"Because you are the best for several reasons, your name Chameleon says it all. You can blend into any level of society, high society in this case. O'Reilly loves the celebrity status; aristocracy, politicians, film and TV stars all attend his lavish gatherings. He craves recognition at the top strata. He has been married three times, he is now 49 years of age, his first marriage was when he was in his 20s, lasted seven years, his wife died of a drug overdose. It is suspected that she had become an embarrassment and was a block to his ambitions. For the last two years, he attended social events on his own. Was she murdered? Highly likely.

By then, he was a gang boss, suspected of organising hi-jacking of vehicles carrying all type of goods, robberies of jewellery shops, also dabbling in the drugs trade then. He was an admirer of the Krays; they had moved in the top level of society, socialising with politicians, film and TV actresses and actors. His second marriage was to a model, an aspiring one, not at the top level but close. That lasted five years, she disappeared when they were on a yacht, sailing in the Aegean, her body was never recovered. Was she murdered? Again, very likely."

Huntsman stared at Marlowe and continued, "He married a third time four years ago, the marriage is disintegrating, it is only a matter of time before something tragic happens to her. Her maiden name was Susan Danson."

At the mention of the name Marlowe jerked his head, "Sue is his third wife?"

"Yes, you were intimately involved with her about six years ago, I never did know what caused the split."

"The bloody job was the cause, I broke our relationship because I did not want her to become a widow; it was a bloody unhappy time. Sue was bitter about it, she walked out and since that awful night we have never been in contact. You are a cunning bastard, springing this on me."

"You still have much affection for her, yes.?"

"You know the answer."

"So, you will accept the assignment?"

"You know the answer to that too, I wish to make something clear, this is my last assignment, apart from any reward and insurance pay off, how much are you paying me?"

"A quarter of a million."

"Not enough, the job warrants much more, I am putting my life and Sue's life on the line, make me a better offer?"

"Half a million."

"I want 50 per cent of that paid into a bank account before I make one move."

Huntsman sighed. "Very well." He grinned and handed Marlowe a bank statement, it was a statement of one of Marlowe's accounts showing a deposit of 250,000 pounds entered into the account yesterday.

Marlowe stared at the account and despite himself, a wry grin appeared on his face, "You really are a devious bastard, you knew I would take the job?"

"I was pretty certain; I am sure you have retained affection for Susan O'Reilly and that you will make every effort to stop any harm to her."

"Is that the only reason you want me to do this job?"

"No, I did state that you are the best-you are lethal; you never hesitate to pull the trigger you can infiltrate at any level, get close to the target despite how much protection he has surrounding him."

"So is it a 'Wanted dead or alive' case?"

"If you can trace where the proceeds of the robberies are, be it offshore accounts or hidden in deposit boxes, whatever, everyone would prefer O'Reilly to end up in a coffin."

Huntsman handed Marlowe a folder, "This is a dossier giving details of O'Reilly, his antecedence, his associates, his minders, who he socialises with, photographs of various people and of his villa. His likes and dislikes, study it and memorise it, either return it to me or destroy it. He has regular parties at his villa. Marbella is a jet set destination, there are always celebrities on vacation there or who reside there, most of them do attend his lavish gatherings; he regards this as acceptance at the top strata of society. His right hand man, Brown, is suspected of a number of killings, he is a brute, big in stature, an ugly bastard but as cunning as a fox, be very wary of him."

Marlowe was given a second folder, "Here are details of your cover, your identity, you are now Malcom McColl, sole offspring, son and heir of the Earl of Sutherland. The earl has advanced dementia, he has a full-time male nurse who takes care of him. He did have a son who died when an infant. His wife died several years ago. The estate is the largest in Scotland, actually, the largest in Britain. It is managed by a board of trustees set up by the earl when he was diagnosed with the illness. When he dies, the estate will go to the Scottish National Trust. The earl is a multi-millionaire, reckoned to be the wealthiest aristocrat in Britain. You have a reputation as a playboy, a bachelor, one of the jet set, your haunts being Monaco, Biarritz, St Moritz, Bahamas and other places.

You can make up more stories of your antecedence. Society magazines have been given snippets of your reputation. That even though you are a playboy you consider your privacy as sacrosanct and will have nothing to do with the media. You are very discreet and do not give interviews."

Marlowe checked the contents of the folder, in an envelope were credit cards, an ATM card and a wad of banknotes, sterling and euros plus a driving licence all in the name of Malcom McColl. He said, "I will need a passport in that name?"

"No doubt you will wish to alter your appearance, when you have done so, forward passport photographs to me and a passport will be issued; give me a call and a courier will collect the photographs and the passport will be delivered to you in the same manner. After you receive the passport, let me know you are ready to proceed with the assignment. Either you or I can arrange a flight to Malaga, just let me know so I can arrange that you are met at the airport by your contact.

Diego Garcia is a Guardia Civil officer stationed in Marbella; he has been investigating O'Reilly but in an undercover capacity. He is working alone; he cannot trust any other officer or any of the Marbella town police. A number of police officers are hired to check guests at O'Reilly's gatherings, no doubt well compensated for their moonlighting. Garcia has pinpointed warehouses in the area which he suspects is where the transport is kept for the drugs. The premises are always closed, patrolled by security 24 hours, surrounded by a 15-feet high chain fence topped by several strands of razor wire. He has never gained access to see what is inside, he will tell you everything he has done and what he suspects. You can rely on him one hundred per cent. He will supply you with the weapon or weapons of your choice.

You do have a problem, if his wife recognises you, what will be her reaction? If O'Reilly suspects that you know each other, he will dig until he gets the facts then he will know that you are an imposter."

"I will adopt a guise which I am certain will work, at least confuse her. I will have passport photos taken tomorrow, once you send me the passport I can leave for Spain."

"I'll be ready by then, give me a contact number so I can pass info."

Huntsman wrote a telephone number. "My private number, contact me any time, day or night, I look forward to hearing from you."

Wolf returned and Huntsman left. In the car, Wolf remarked, "Do you think he will get results; did you tell him about the fate of Badger and Otter, that we do not know about what happened to them, only that they are missing?"

"No, I saw no good reason to tell him and as I said he is the best, I should have contacted him six months ago instead of sending the two operatives who are no doubt dead." Wolf thought, *Boss, you are a cold-hearted bastard.*

Preparations

As soon as they had left, Marlowe went to the cellar, pulled a wine rack to one side, he then pushed a section of wall which swung open, he took out two metal cases, closed the wall opening and put the wine rack into its correct position. He went upstairs. The first case he opened contained many items of disguise. Hairpieces, beards, moustaches, contact lenses of different shades, false noses and ears, various cosmetic makeup. He selected very clear blue contact lenses, inserted them, he viewed the result in a mirror, and was satisfied. From several pairs of sunglasses, he chose two pairs with mirror lenses.

The second case contained several handguns, knives and other items. He took out a double edged ceramic knife, as sharp as a razor, in a sheath which had straps, it could be attached to a forearm or an ankle. A small but very powerful pair of binoculars was taken also a powerful pencil sized torch. He put the cases back into the recess and replaced the wine rack. He took the items to his bedroom where he picked out the clothes he would wear specially for night operations. Two sets of black lightweight slacks, black long sleeved shirts, waist length bomber'style jacket, black balaclava, black ski mask, paper thin black gloves, socks, trainers, belt, all black. He packed all the articles into a compact holdall. He then picked out the attire he would wear in his role. Smart casual wear, short-sleeved shirts, chino pants, one lightweight pale blue linen jacket plus the accessories-underwear, shoes etc. These were packed in a second holdall. In his carry-on-flight bag, he placed a Stephen Leather novel, a *Daily Telegraph* crossword book, biro pens, pencils, a pack of tissues, a packet of mint sweets. He double-checked all the items, secured the holdalls with padlocks. He then popped a macaroni and cheese meal into the microwave, brewed coffee and then read the dossiers. After his meal, he read the dossiers until he had memorised them, he then burnt them in the open fireplace of the lounge.

The weather was clear, no sign of rain; he donned motorcycle protective clothing and took out the machine. He rode to Glenrothes, a 15 to 20 minute ride. He parked inside the vehicle park at the shopping centre, left the helmet and jacket secured to the motorcycle, jacket in a locked pannier, helmet chained to the handlebars. The first premises he visited was a unisex hairdresser's. He had a trim and his hair dyed blonde, including his eyebrows, he purchased packets of the dye. He then visited a photographer where he had passport photos taken. He returned home.

He had decided to pose as a casual, uninterested individual in current affairs, perceived as foppish, modelled on the fictional characters *The Scarlet Pimpernel* and *Zorro* which as a boy he had seen films of their exploits. He practised a certain way of walking and moving, a languid movement bordering on but not quite effeminate. He worked on this for some considerable time until it became his natural manner. He phoned Huntsman, "I have the passport photos, I am fully prepared, when I get the passport I can leave."

"A courier will collect them in 30 minutes, the passport should be delivered tomorrow. I will arrange your flight and transportation to the airport." The courier collected the photos. After he left, Marlowe practised his mode of speech which was a refined Highland accent, soft with a lilt; eventually, with his style of walk and accent when both were natural and he had assumed his character change, he relaxed and prepared a meal, he thought about the assignment and the challenge it posed, particularly about Sue. They had an intense relationship for two years, living together. It had been a bitter break-up but he had been totally involved in his work which had been extremely perilous most of the time. He now regretted his decision; he had been deeply in love and still harboured strong feelings, he intended to save her from whatever fate O'Reilly intended and anyone who obstructed him would pay the penalty.

Morning

He was up at the crack of dawn at around 5 a.m. He had breakfast, checked his baggage, ensured that the garage was secure and watched the TV news. He unlocked the gate on the driveway and awaited the courier. Just before 11 a.m., he heard a car which stopped outside the front door. He opened the door to find Huntsman standing there. Wolf was sitting in the driver's seat. "Come in," spoken in his new accent, Huntsman followed, noting Marlowe's style of movement.

"I must say your guise is first class, it would have fooled me if I had seen you elsewhere." He handed over the passport, Marlowe checked the details. "You have a direct flight with Ryanair departure 4.40 p.m. from Edinburgh, first class, arrives at Malaga at 8 p.m. Accommodation is reserved at the Hotel El Faro, not the most expensive hotel but the location is in the centre of Marbella, reserved provisionally for two weeks with an option to stay longer. All paid for, if you have to stay longer, you will be reimbursed."

"Sounds good."

"There is something else I should have told you; Wolf mentioned it yesterday, I wasn't going to tell you as I did not want to sidetrack you from your main objective. On reflection, I was wrong, I should have told you. About six months ago, I sent two operatives on the assignment you are now undertaking, they got nowhere, nothing of any use from them, two weeks later nary a word, nothing and I have not received any news about them since, they have disappeared, no trace, hotel rooms cancelled, their belongings removed. It is certain that they have been killed."

"Who did you send?"

"Badger and Otter."

"Shit, I knew Otter, he was a good guy, smart and efficient; Badger not so much but I heard he was pretty good as well, this won't deter me but if I ever discover who did them in, I will take action."

"I knew what your answer would be, primary object, stop the drug trafficking, achieve that then you can wipe out anyone involved and I would like to know who killed my men. Any reward will be yours; I wish you all the best, transport to the airport at 1.30 p.m. Tickets and hotel details are in this envelope. I hope to hear something positive from you soon." Huntsman left.

Spain

The flight touched down after 8.15 p.m. He collected his two holdalls and entered the arrivals hall. He saw a man holding a large piece of cardboard with 'Sutherland' printed on it. He crossed over and said in perfect Spanish, "Senor Garcia?"

"Si" was the reply, Garcia was about 5 feet 10 inches tall, medium build, clean shaven, black curly hair, dark complexion, he reminded Marlowe of the film actor Antonio Banderos. Dressed in jeans, white shirt, waist-length brown leather jacket and cowboy boots with two-inch heels. Garcia said in English, "My car is parked about 150 metres away, use a trolley for your bags."

"Your English is perfect."

"My mother is English, my father Spanish, I was born in London. My father was an official in the Spanish Embassy. I went to English schools. It is best if we converse in English, I know you speak Spanish but there are more Spanish citizens here than English and one never knows who is listening."

Garcia paid the parking fee; his car was a seat model Toledo a large saloon type. Once the journey started Garcia said, "What did your boss tell you about me?"

"That you were reliable, that you could not trust fellow officers, that you had located warehouses but had not affected entry, you suspect the warehouses are used to load drugs into vehicles, the destination being England."

"That is true, in the door side pocket, there is a large-scale map of Andalucia, the red crosses on it show where the warehouses are sited. The blue crosses show the likely spots where the speed boats land the drugs."

Marlowe scanned the map, "Describe the warehouses and their locations to me?"

"All are in the countryside, a single track lane leads to them and goes no further, they are only two storeys in height, windows only on the upper floor. No other living quarters within a mile all round, only a few ruined houses. The ground has been cleared for a distance of about 100 metres, surrounding every warehouse, a security gatehouse is about 50 metres from the warehouse manned by two guards. Four-metre high chain link fences with several strands of razor wire surround the buildings, security lighting at every corner. The guards are armed with pump shotguns, they have sidearms as well. The buildings are large enough to garage six large vehicles."

"Quite a well-organised outfit, are the fences electrified?"

"I am not certain but I do not think so. I have watched from a distance; I did not see any dead wildlife on the ground on either side of the fence."

"It is important to see inside the buildings, any ideas?"

"I have never seen the guards patrol around the warehouses, their blind spot is the rear but the entry into the buildings is in full view of them."

"How long is their tour of duty?"

"Twelve hours, 6 a.m. to 6 p.m. then 6 p.m. to 6 a.m."

"They must eat and drink during the 12 hours, do they have cooking facilities or do they have food delivered?"

"They probably have a microwave but two times I saw a Pizza Hut motorcyclist deliver to the guardhouses at two locations."

Marlowe was deep in thought and silent for a few minutes then he said, "It is vital that I gain entry into at least one warehouse; to do that the guards have to be put out of action temporary. I will need your assistance, my idea is for takeaway food to be spiked with a strong sedative, put them to sleep. You will deliver the food, they will say they never ordered, your reply will be that you made a mistake and delivered it to the wrong guardhouse, hopefully they will take the food despite your protests that it has to be delivered to another location. There are no risks involved but it all depends on their taking the food. What do you think?'

"It could work, as you say, there is no risk, in fact, we could carry it out at more than one locale, I can get a very strong sedative from a pharmacist I know. May I speak frankly?"

"Of course."

"When I saw you at the airport, I was not impressed, your appearance and manner worried me but now I think you are very smart and we can work well together."

Marlowe smiled, "You suspected that I had a questionable gender, the saying 'First impressions are usually correct' does not apply in this instance, I assure you, a few months ago, two operatives were assigned to investigate O'Reilly, a short time after they disappeared, no trace of them since. Did you know them?"

"No, I did hear via the grapevine that there were two men asking questions but I was not working with your organisation then. O'Reilly has a very large yacht moored at Puerto Banus, it very seldom leaves the port but if it does, it returns in a few hours, I think it is used for two purposes mainly, to get rid of bodies and to supervise from a distance the landing of drugs from speed boats."

"I am sure you are right, I do want to know what happened to them. I guess a confession is the only means we will know, when I am certain who knows something I will extract an admission and the facts and I will use any means to get at the truth." Diego glanced at Marlowe's expression, saw the cold, grimness and thought, *God help them, this is one tough hombre.*

He said, "What do I call you?"

"Now, I am called Malcom McColl so call me Malcom or Mal."

Diego laughed, "I think Malo would suit you but I call you Mal."

They arrived at the hotel, Diego said, "I won't come in, best that we are not seen together. For meetings, there is a small bar two streets away, only Spanish patrons, it is called El Caballero, I will see you there at noon tomorrow."

"Diego, I want to hire a motorcycle, is there a dealer near here?"

"There are three dealers in the town, all reliable, any taxi driver can take you, adios for now."

Marlowe picked up his baggage and entered the hotel. He went to the reception desk;, two very attractive women were on duty. He said, "I am Senor McColl, I have a reservation." He handed his passport to a beautiful woman, early 30s, black hair in a long ponytail tied with a red velvet bow, on her blouse pocket was pinned a nametag 'Maria'.

"Senor you have one of our best suites." She took the passport to photocopy it, she returned the passport and he signed registration forms. She then said, "Come with me please,' she summoned an employee to carry the baggage. They exited the elevator on the fourth floor, she led the way, inserted a key card and opened the door, the baggage was taken into a spacious bedroom and the employee left. Maria showed him the suite, bathroom, a safe inside the wardrobe, a smart 50-inch TV, a mini- fridge packed with alcoholic and soft drinks. She opened the French doors leading onto a large terrace which had a table and chairs. She showed him how to dim all the lights, the furniture was modern of a good quality.

He said, "Very nice, I will be very comfortable here, thank you for showing me."

"You are welcome, if there is anything you want just call me." She smiled, her eyes twinkling.

"Anything?"

"Yes, Senor, anything." He surmised whether it was a double entendre.

" May I call you Maria?"

"Yes, of course."

"Maria, forgive me for being impulsive, you are very beautiful, I would be honoured if you would accompany me on your night off. I wish to take you for an excellent meal and to talk, drink and have a very nice evening."

"I like it very much. Two nights from now, I do not work, I will not meet you here but I see you at The Mirador restaurant, it is on the beach road, at 8.30 p.m. okay?"

"Yes, I will look forward to it." She left the room.

It had been a considerable period since he had a relationship with a woman; he had been a recluse for months, now he found himself looking forward to taking her out, for her company, if it ended in intimacy, good and well but he would never push matters, it would be up to her if she desired to take things further.

The First Day

He rose early and went for breakfast which was a first-class buffet, he read a local English newspaper and saw a short article on page three, it merely stated that the heir of the Earl of Sutherland was visiting Marbella and hoped that he would enjoy his trip and return often. The receptionist called for a taxi; Marlowe asked the driver to take him to a good motorcycle hire dealer. Five minutes later, he was dropped off at a large showroom. There was a great variety of motorcycles for hire, he opted for a lightweight Honda, 125 cc automatic. Power and speed was not a requisite for him; he wished to travel around and view the countryside at a modest pace without having to engage foot gears. A helmet was included, so he picked one with a tinted visor. He hired the machine for two weeks, paid the price plus a deposit.

Before heading out of town, he scanned the map that Diego had given him. The nearest warehouse was about four kilometres away, three kilometres north on the Carretera which paralleled the coast and then a turn left onto a side road, one kilometre further was the warehouse. He stopped some 500 metres from it and viewed it with his binoculars. It was exactly how Diego described it. The doors closed, no activity, he could only see someone sitting in the guardhouse. He visited two more warehouses, similar scenarios. At 11.30, he rode back to town. Parked the machine in the hotel parking garage. He then walked to the El Caballero and went inside. Diego was sitting at a table reading a newspaper, drinking a coffee. Marlowe sat opposite him and ordered a Cafe Leche.

"I had a scout around and viewed three warehouses, no sign of any activity or vehicles parked outside, have you any idea how often the drug runs take place?"

"Not exactly sure but I hear whispers that two times a month the boats land the drugs. Large consignments, 100s of kilos the street value must be many millions of euros. No one to stop them, the Guardia nowhere near." "

You suspect that the cops are dirty?"

"Yes and it must be someone high up who gives orders and designates the areas to patrol, areas well away from the landing spots. In a few days, there will be a drugs run but I do not know where they will be landed."

Marlowe was deep in thought for moments then he said, "It is obvious that you have informants, all the best cops have their snouts. I don't want to know who they are but I do want to know when the drugs are landed. My plan is this, it is essential that I get into the warehouses before the drugs are landed. I want to photograph the vehicles and any documents, I will text the details and photos to my boss. The drugs will be landed and taken to the warehouses. We let the drugs be transferred into the vehicles and to go on their journeys. When they reach England, they will be followed to their destinations, then and only then will the drugs squads take action. The organisation will take a massive hit. I will then tackle O'Reilly and his men. What is your opinion?"

Diego was silent, "I think it is a good plan, we do not have the manpower to deal with vehicles here and destroying them in England is best. I do have people here who will give me information and I should know when the drugs are landed. When do we get into the warehouses?"

"Tomorrow night before 9 p.m., the guards will be feeling hungry, so you deliver pizzas then."

Diego grinned, "Fantastic."

"Have you ever met O'Reilly and his number one man, Joseph Brown?"

"No, O'Reilly only leaves his villa to go out on his yacht when there is a drug run. I have seen and heard about Brown. he has a reputation, a violent man who enjoys inflicting pain. He is a big man, tall with a big body, shaven head, red face. He is at O'Reilly's side always when outside the villa but O'Reilly comes into town alone some nights to visit a bordello. He pays big money or the girls will not go with him, he is a sadist, a sexual monster who likes to whip the girls."

"Surely, the bordello owner has men to protect his girls?"

"Everyone is frightened of Brown and O'Reilly and of course, the money Brown pays compensates the owner and the girls."

"I hear O'Reilly is married, have you seen his wife?"

"No, she stays at the villa most of the time, I was told that anytime she leaves the villa, two of his men stay with her. I have never seen her but I believe she was a very beautiful woman once, now she is thin and looks terrible, I was told that she is a junkie."

Marlowe felt a terrible cold rage, O'Reilly and his gang of thugs would suffer intense pain before they would be dispatched. His eyes were like glaciers, he said, "O'Reilly was married twice before, both wives died or were killed."

Diego said, "Rumours are that O'Reilly has a mistress, a Russian woman, who visits him at his villa. I think his wife will disappear soon."

"We meet here at the same time tomorrow, will you check your informants, any information will be useful. Diego, we will destroy these evil bastards, failure is not an option."

Diego saw the cold look and thought, *he is right, we will smash them.* Marlowe then left and returned to the hotel. As he entered reception, one of the receptionists waved at him, he went to the desk and was handed an envelope which he opened. It was an invitation to a social gathering at El Rancho at 8 p.m. Reception and welcome drink at 7.30 p.m. The location was marked on the card. On the back he read, 'Dear Mr McColl, I would be honoured by your presence, I assure you, you will have a wonderful time,' signed D O'Reilly. He thought tonight was when he would put on an Oscar-winning act. He was feeling peckish, so he went to a nearby bar where there was a variety of tapas. He selected a number of them and had a Cruzcampo beer. He pondered about how matters were now escalating but he was really concerned about Sue. He doubted whether she would attend the social if she was in a drugged condition, even if she did she would not recognise him in her befuddled condition. After leaving the bar, he had a stroll around the town, visiting the famous Plaza de Naranjas where many tourists were having refreshments not minding the inflated tourist prices. He was back at the hotel just after 5 p.m.

Maria was on duty; she gave him a big smile. "Buenas tardes, Maria, ¿estás bien."

"Si, Señor, your Spanish is very good."

"Thank you, I speak a little of your language, I hope to learn more shortly," and he smiled.

She replied, "I am sure you will," accompanied by a smile. He went to his room to relax before the night's event.

The Social Gathering

Marlowe got ready for the night's event, dressed smart casually, short sleeved open neck plain light blue shirt, beige chinos, slip on light moccasin style shoes, no socks. He locked his cell phone in the safe, he did not carry any identification, only the invitation card. He went to reception and handed his room keycard to Maria, she said, "Have a nice evening, Senor."

"That is debatable, it could be called an appointment with destiny; see you later."

Outside there were taxis lined up opposite, he got into one and gave instructions, "El Rancho villa, Senor O'Reilly's, do you know where it is?"

"Si, I know." It was only a 10-minute drive along the Ojen road and then a turn right onto a private road leading to the villa. He requested a card from the driver, "What time do you finish?"

"In the morning about 2 to 3 a.m."

"I will give you a call later." He paid the fare plus a tip.

"Gracias, I come for you later."

He assumed the affected manner of walking and approached the columned entrance which had double doors, both closed, outside were two men in plain clothes. They stepped in front of him, one said, "We search you."

Marlowe replied, "You can see that I am not carrying anything but if it gives you a thrill to manhandle me, go ahead and enjoy it." Both men recoiled, disdainful facial expressions. One did a cursory pat down as if Marlowe had an infectious disease and opened the door, Marlowe glimpsed the other guard making a gesture with a hand to indicate what he thought Marlowe was. Inside there was a desk and cloakroom, a pretty girl dressed in a French maid's dress but scantier, requested his invitation card. He handed it over; she spoke into a type of pager. The door at the end of the hallway opened and two men came out. One was a large figure; Marlowe knew that this was Brown. The other he assumed was O'Reilly held his hand out, Marlowe shook it in a limp manner. Brown had a disgusted expression.

O'Reilly said, "I am so pleased to meet you and that you came to our little party, what do I call you?"

"Your honour or your highness but, sir will do."

O'Reilly was taken aback, the smile on his face vanished. Marlowe giggled, "I'm joking, just call me Malcom."

"Malcom you had me there, welcome to the party, enjoy yourself. There are many beautiful girls here if they are to your taste, good food, plenty of drinks and bedrooms upstairs if you are inclined that way."

"Oh, I enjoy girls as well. Thank you for inviting me." The three of them entered a huge sitting room with a bar on one side and a long table laden with food on the opposite side, settees and armchairs in abundance. O'Reilly took him to the bar, "Just name your drink and my man will fix it."

"A Tequila Sunrise if you please."

O'Reilly and Brown moved away, Brown commented, "He's a fucking poof, why did you invite him?"

"Joe, he is heir to fucking billions, his old man will snuff it soon, if we get some interesting pictures of him, we can squeeze his balls so hard that his fucking eyes will pop. Get my drift?"

"I would love to stick a few needles in him and a red hot poker up his arse."

"When we get all his cash, you can do what you like."

Marlowe was moving around, viewing the scene; there was no sign of Sue. Activities in many cases were getting hot and steamy, twosomes and threesomes were entwined on the settees. Clothing being discarded. At the end of the room, there were open French doors leading onto a terrace and a large oval swimming pool, discreet lighting surrounded the pool and gardens. There were couples in the pool, naked, engaged sexually, one girl was leaning with her elbows on the side whilst a guy was having intercourse. By the sounds both were uttering, their climaxes would occur any second. A man was sitting on the side, his legs in the water as a girl administered fellatio. Marlowe recognised a few faces, a couple of rising film starlets, a pop star, a politician. He wandered back inside, a very pretty girl, late teens or early 20s, topless and only wearing a thong came up to him and flung her arms around his neck and rubbed herself against him, she slurred her words, "I want to be fucked, any hole you want."

Marlowe said, "Sober up and I will consider it, I do not fuck drunks."

She pouted and said, "Fuck you," and left him.

He explored further, came across a staircase leading to a long terrace with several doors. He strolled along the terrace; he heard voices from some of the rooms, all of a sexual nature judging from the sounds emitting. At the end room, he heard screams, O'Reilly bustled to him, "I think someone is in trouble in there," he said.

O'Reilly answered, "Malcom, there is no problem, my wife is having bad dreams that is all."

"Sorry for intruding, I did not realise you were married." Marlowe turned and left as a statuesque blonde woman passed him on the terrace going towards O'Reilly, he heard her say, "Darling, is she making trouble for you?"

"No big deal, Tanya, I'll give her something to quiet her down."

He met Brown at the bottom of the stairs who said, "Snooping around, you can get into bother doing that."

"Oh dear, big man, no doubt you would like to give the punishment, isn't it time you came out of the closet?"

Brown's face flushed red, he looked like he was having apoplexy, he spluttered his words, "You fucking little shit, I would break you in half but the boss thinks you are something special, fuck knows why."

Marlowe simpered, "Don't worry, big man, you're not my type, too coarse actually. You stick to the sweaty labouring type, definitely more to your taste." He laughed as he walked off leaving Brown clenching his fists.

Unknown to both adversaries, one of the male servants in the shadows had seen the exchange and heard most of it. The servant, a Spaniard in his late 30s was more interested in Marlowe; he was intrigued in the baiting of Brown whom he detested with a vehement passion. The servant made a discreet enquiry with the cloakroom girl who only knew Marlowe's alias, and that she had never seen him here before.

Marlowe had seen enough; he sought out O'Reilly and told him he was leaving, that he was tired from jet lag, he thanked him for the invitation and that he hoped he would be considered for any future social event. He requested that someone call for a taxi, he handed the taxi driver's card to O'Reilly who passed it on to a servant with the request. He left then and pursed a kiss at the two guards as he went by to wait in the road, 15 minutes later the taxi arrived.

It was only 10.30 when he arrived at the hotel, he went to reception to get his keycard. Maria was the sole receptionist, she gave it to him and remarked, "An early night? Most guests do not return until the morning from El Rancho."

He answered her question with a question, "You knew where I was?"

"I guessed, Marbella is like a village, much gossip and talk among the Spanish people."

"Maria, I am a very private person, discretion is my motto, the type of gathering I attended was not to my liking. I am not prudish, if people like to exhibit their desires in front of others, it is up to them."

She said, "I am pleased, Malcom, can I call you Malcom if that is your name?"

"Yes, of course, Malcolm is fine."

She looked seriously at him, "I have a feeling that you are not a playboy that the newspapers say you are."

He said, "Please keep your thoughts to yourself, we will have a good talk the night after tomorrow. I can tell you a little about myself but not everything. I want to know much about you, forgive me for being candid, I am attracted to you and I hope you feel a little of the same about me."

She smiled sweetly and said, "I am interested in you and I am attracted, you are a man of mystery which always appeals."

He grinned. "I hope it is more than that, goodnight, Maria." He went to his room, many thoughts in his head, Sue, Brown, O'Reilly and last but not least, Maria. It was some time before he fell asleep,

The Second Morning

Marlowe rose later than usual, he had a full breakfast, fresh fruit, bacon, eggs, mushrooms, hash browns, tomatoes, toast, orange juice, coffee; he took his time savouring it. He then sat in the lounge and perused English newspapers, both broadsheets and tabloids. He was particularly interested in any reports pertaining to drugs. One well written article in *The Times* referred to the growing numbers of addicts and the many crimes committed by drug users. It published the alarming statistics and the suspected sources of the drugs. France, the Marseilles connection, Corsica, Sicily, Morocco, Algiers, Andorra were all mentioned, media speculation as usual.

At about noon, he walked to El Caballero to meet Diego who was sitting at the same table, Diego called to the bartender, "Dos café con leche por favor."

Diego smiled, "Did you enjoy yourself last night?"

Marlowe smiled. "It seems there are no secrets in this town, let's say it served a purpose, 'Know thy enemies' is an old saying but a very true one."

"You really made an enemy of Brown; he wants to injure you very badly."

"I guess one of your informants told you, I can handle him and I intend to break every bone I can think of in that evil body." Diego saw the icy glint in Marlowe's eyes and did not doubt that Brown's fate was sealed.

He said, "I am ready for tonight, I have a Pizza Hut jacket and one of their motorcycles with the box. I have a very strong sedative, tasteless, after taking it will take only 15 to 20 minutes to knock them out, they will not wake up for many hours, four or five at least."

"Great, we can take our time and ensure that we do not miss anything, deliver the first lot about 9 p.m. I will follow you but will wait just off the Carretera on the approach road. I will wait for your word."

"Your missing colleagues were last seen in Puerto Banus a few months ago, shortly after O'Reilly's boat was seen leaving the port. Brown was on board with several of his men, there is little doubt that your guys were killed and dumped at sea."

"I have no doubt that you are right. A pity a person can only die once, I wish Brown could pay many times over."

"Diego, I know nothing about your personal life, do you have a lady friend, fiancé or wife?"

"I have a wife, Dulcena, and two children, a boy called Ramon, six years and a daughter, Teresa, three years. They live in Granada; we have an apartment there. I manage to go there every two weeks for a few days. I love it there; it is a beautiful city and I adore my wife and children. I am teaching my children to ski, Dulcena and I are good skiers, it is wonderful in the Winter."

"I envy you very much, I have often thought that I would love to have a family life; six years ago I had been in a relationship with a beautiful lady but because of my profession, I broke up with her and I have regretted it ever since. I am getting on a bit now so as the time passes the likelihood of having a normal family life is more and more unlikely."

"Mal, my friend, it is not too late for you; you are a fit, good-looking man, I believe in fate, that relationship was never meant to be, you will meet someone I am truly certain and that both of you will have a wonderful, loving life together." Marlowe looked at Diego and had a fleeting thought that he knew about Maria, he then dismissed it.

"I hope you are right; I am getting tired of my way of life." They chatted for a little longer and then left the bar. Marlowe went to the hotel and relaxed in his room for the rest of the afternoon.

Night Activities

Marlowe dressed in all black phoned Diego, "I will park near Pizza Hut, it is the one in the main street right? I will be there before 8.30." Diego confirmed the location. Marlowe left the hotel, handed the keycard to Maria who gave him a quizzical look but did not make any comment, he gave her a smile, "If I don't see you later, I will see you tomorrow night." He left and motorcycled to a spot near the restaurant. He saw Diego come out with two large plastic containers which he placed in the box fixed behind the pillion seat; Diego saw him and nodded. Marlowe followed him and they left the town on the Malaga Road.

When Diego entered the side road, Marlowe followed for about 50 yards and parked. More than 30 minutes later, Diego phoned him, "Come now." He reached the gate which was ajar. Diego was there; he said, "Both are sleeping, I have the key for the warehouse." Inside the building were two articulated lorries and two pantechnicons. Using his smartphone, Marlowe took pictures of the vehicles and close-ups of the registration numbers. He then searched all the cabs and photographed every piece of paper or document. One document intrigued him, each cab had the identical document; it was a duty rota showing dates and tours of duty for someone called B O'Donnell, it was a printed, form on the bottom there was a handwritten sentence, "Make sure you arrive when B is on duty." He showed the document to Diego, "What do you make of this?"

"I think there is a crooked official who allows the trucks to go through without any examination of their loads."

"That is exactly what I think. I think he must be the customs officer in charge at the Calais end of the channel tunnel; there is no check when they reach England. O'Donnell is an Irish surname; I wager O'Reilly and him have a past history."

There was a small cubicle serving as an office in the premises, Marlowe photographed everything there. "Okay, Diego, I've got everything, on to the next one." The warehouse was locked and the key returned to the guardhouse. The gates were secured by a self-locking padlock, no key was required to secure the lock.

Two other locations were visited, the same plan was successful, six other different types of trucks were photographed and the same duty rota was found in every cab. Every vehicle was painted in the same colours, yellow and green, all bearing the same words Andalucia Fine Foods Export Co.

They returned to Marbella and stopped at a bar in a side street. It was a late-night one and served food. Boquerones, tortilla and meatballs were ordered and pints of San Miguel draught beer. Both men were feeling hungry and the food was eaten in no time. Marlowe said, "Diego, that was a good night's work, I will pass the information on to my boss; he will do the necessary at Calais and England. Now all we want is for the drug run to take place, for the vehicles to be loaded for their journeys to England, I reckon each truck will have two drivers so from here it should not take longer than 36 hours to reach Calais."

"Mal, what about other ports, Cherbourg, Le Havre and Dunkirk all have ferry services to England?"

"No way, the vehicles will arrive when O'Donnell is on duty, once passed through, they can end up in different locations in England. The street value of the drugs will be hundreds of million euros. O'Reilly will have to pay several million up front, when he finds out that all the vehicles have been seized he will go crazy. That is when I make the final moves."

"Do you have any plans to deal with Brown and O'Reilly?"

"At the moment, nothing specific, can you get me a 9 milligram handgun, any make as long as it functions well and also a good suppressor?"

"No problem, how many magazines?"

"Four or Five will be sufficient."

"I want to be there when you tackle them."

"Diego, amigo, thank you for your offer but the final jobs, I do alone. I do not want to risk you getting injured or God forbid getting killed. At the final stage of any operation. I work alone. I do not have to worry about anyone else, I can focus better. I don't wish to offend you, please understand."

Diego gave a little smile, "I understand, please be careful, my friend. I think you have killed before."

"More times than I can remember. I have no conscience or guilt, all were evil, lethal scum who did not deserve to live. O'Reilly and Brown are of the same ilk, they will die and any of their men who try to obstruct me." Diego felt a cold shiver, he had never ever fired his firearm on duty at any criminal yet the man sitting opposite was a multiple killer, an assassin who killed without compassion. "Mal, I will bring the weapon and ammo to you tomorrow, same time and place."

"Great, let's have another beer and then it's off to bed."

It was well after midnight when Marlowe got back to the hotel. Maria handed him his keycard, "You look a little tired, did you have a good night?"

"I would call it a successful night."

She raised her eyebrows, "Maria, I would like to tell you all about it and perhaps one day, I will but now my bed is calling for me."

She gave him a big smile. "One day, I will remind you to tell me about your mysterious nights in Marbella."

"That sounds ideal, goodnight, lovely lady." She watched him walk away and thought, I *want to know everything about you, who and what you are, you are a mystery and I am getting more and more interested and I am attracted to you, I hope it is mutual and that it develops.*

Huntsman

As soon as he closed the door, Marlowe called Huntsman. "Good evening or is it morning? I did not expect any contact from you this early." Marlowe briefed him on everything that had occurred, what he had discovered in the warehouses, his visit at the social gathering, the information and assumed fate of Badger and Otter. He told him that he would send all that he had recorded on his phone. "Garcia, who incidentally is a first-class guy, is sure there will be a drug run soon, within the next two or three days. May I suggest that they be allowed to continue to their destinations in England shadowed by your agents and/or the drug squads, hit them then and capture the lot? That should destroy the network once all the prisoners have been interrogated. The corrupt customs officer, O'Donnell, can be arrested later."

"I concur with your plan, I will liaise with all the necessary authorities, what about O'Reilly, Brown and his men in Spain.?"

"I will deal with them, as our cousins say, with extreme prejudice."

"What about Susan, have you seen her?"

"No, but from what I have heard, she is a junkie, in very bad health and I suspect will be disposed of soon."

"I am so dreadfully sorry to hear that, is there any hope she will recover?"

"From what I hear, I doubt it, she is so far gone."

Huntsman was silent and then he said, "I truly wish I had brought you in much earlier, I kept away from you as long as I could."

"I am glad I undertook this assignment; I will exact my brand of justice for Sue, Badger and Otter, no one will escape."

"Good, when it is over, we will meet when you come back to England; in such a short time, you have obtained extraordinary results. Hope to hear from you soon, thank you." The call ended and Marlowe mused about Huntsman, the boss had seemed genuinely sorry, perhaps he had a soft spot in that cast iron heart of his.

The Third Day

A day of relaxation, a walk about the town in the morning finding the location of The Mirador restaurant, he had a coffee there, he had the usual meeting with Diego who handed him a plain linen shopping bag, he peeked inside it and saw a Walther PK pistol, suppressor and magazines. There was no information as yet about the drug run. They had tapas and beers and then Marlowe returned to the hotel, he placed the weapon and accessories in the safe. He spent the afternoon by the pool, he swam 40 lengths doing different strokes then visited the hotel fitness room where for an hour he did various exercises.

He went to his room and watched TV until it was time to get ready for his appointment. Shave, shower and then fresh clean clothing. Short sleeved, open neck white shirt, beige linen pants, socks and slip on casual shoes. He thought about Maria and the evening ahead. He was eager for a relationship to develop; he realised he was falling very hard for her and he hoped that she felt the same. He was determined to take things nice and slow. It was a balmy night, so he walked to the restaurant arriving several minutes before the appointed time. He entered and a waiter came up to him, "A table has been reserved for 8.30."

"What name, Sir?"

He realised he did not know her surname and said, "A lady friend, name is Maria."

"Ah si, Senorita Moreno, come please." He followed the waiter to a table next to the wall at the rear, it was adorned with flowers. He ordered a glass of wine and awaited her.

Just after 8.30, he saw her, she was dressed in a flared floral pattern skirt, knee-length, a peasant type top but sleeveless, cut low enough for an inch of cleavage to show, a lace shawl draped round her shoulders, high heel peep toe strappy shoes setting of her shapely legs. She had a stunning figure, narrow waist, perfect sized breasts. Cosmetics expertly applied to her face, her hair was loose, pearl earrings. She had a lovely smile for him, he stood up, he was almost speechless but managed to utter, "Maria, you are a stunning vision of beauty."

She said, "Malcom, I did not know you were a poet."

He laughed, "The sight of you inspires words."

She sat down opposite him; he asked her to order the wine and whatever other drinks she wanted. A bottle of Rioja red and a bottle of Navarra white were ordered plus a vodka Martini for her. Marlowe stayed with drinking wine. She said, "We eat first, then we talk okay?" The food was ordered, no starter for her, she ordered roast chicken in a mushroom sauce, no potatoes but with broccoli, spinach and okra. He ordered fried Camembert as a starter, lemon sole in a butter and lemon sauce with boiled potatoes, peas, carrots and mushrooms. They ate their food with gusto and chit chatted about it. She declined a dessert, he had blueberry cheesecake, when the coffees arrived, she said, "Now we talk, Malcolm, I want to know many things about you then I talk about myself. Okay?"

"Maria, I never talk about myself but I will to you, I want to know about you too so much, so here goes. I am 43 years old, born in October, I do not know the day because I was abandoned when I was only a day or two old. I was left outside the entrance to a hospital in Glasgow. A blanket wrapped around me. I do not know the name of my mother or father, I was given the name of John Knox, after the famous historic preacher. I was fostered to several families, eventually when I was 11 years old, I was fostered to a very loving couple and I stayed with them until I enlisted in the boys military service I was just under 17 years.

I remained in the army for 12 years, I became a commissioned officer, attaining the rank of Major. I served in many countries, many conflicts. I have a gift for languages, I am fluent in French, German, Russian, Spanish, Castilian, Catalan, Andalucian and I can speak a smattering of Basque. I can converse in Arabic and Chinese. I have several other talents and skills. Before I left the army, I was approached by an organisation, I really cannot give you details but it involved being employed on covert assignments. That is a very sketchy outline. Before you ask, I did try and find out who my mother was, I made enquiries and hired investigators but all were unsuccessful. I used to think about her, why did she abandon me, was it shame being unmarried, was it because she was poor and could not look after me properly, I don't know, it has haunted me all my life, I was not angry or had bad feelings about her, I just wanted to know her." As he spoke about his mother, Maria noticed that his eyes were watery and her heart responded and she felt tearful.

He continued, "I have never married, I did have one long-term relationship which broke up over six years ago, why?

Because my work was dangerous at times and there was always a likelihood of being killed or seriously injured, I did not want to leave her a widow so we broke up, well actually I broke it up, I did love her but she was very upset, was I right or was I wrong, I really do not know the answer."

Maria said, "Surely, it was up to her to decide?"

"You are probably right. I left the organisation over a year ago, became a virtual recluse, I live alone in what was called a hunting lodge in a lovely part of Scotland, I was content, I thought no one knew where I was until my old boss turned up and persuaded me to undertake an assignment. In my profession, I have had many names, many different identities, assumed many different characters but now I just want to lead a nice, quiet life."

"Your assignment is here in Marbella, yes?"

"I cannot answer that but you can guess what it is, it is better you do not know anything that may imperil you. I promise when it is finished I will tell you, it will be over pretty soon. I will get on with my life then, perhaps it is not too late to love someone, to marry and have a family, I live in hope."

She reached across the table and clasped his hand in both of hers, "John, it is not too late, you can and will I am sure, have a very happy, loving future."

"Tell me about yourself, Maria, have you been married?"

"No, I have had two long-term relationships and have had proposals but something just stopped me. John, I am 33 years old, I am not a virgin but I am not what you would call a 'loose woman,' I have wonderful parents who love me and who support my decisions, they live in Malaga, I manage to visit them regularly, I am an only child so perhaps they spoil me, we are Catholics but not strong religiously. I went to Malaga university, got a degree and then did a secretarial course, I have worked in the hotel for over a year. I enjoy my work and I have met the man I want to see more and more."

He looked into her eyes and said, "Maria, my feelings for you grow stronger by the minute, I don't want to rush matters or spoil my chances with you but I want to see you as much as possible. After my assignment is finished, I will return here soon after I have completed the paperwork, you will wait for me?"

She held his hand, "John, you know the answer." He beamed, "I would like to meet your parents."

"You will very soon."

He settled the bill and they left the restaurant, "Shall we get a taxi or can I walk you home?"

"My apartment is only a five minute walk, so we walk." They held hands and she snuggled in close to him as they ambled slowly. They reached the apartment block, at the entrance, they hugged and then went into a tight clinch, he kissed her softly, on her forehead, cheeks, eyes and then on her lips. She responded, her lips parted then opened more as her tongue fenced with his, the kissing became more passionate, they felt the pressure of each other's body, her breasts crushed against his chest, she felt the hardness at his groin. He murmured, "Maria, my darling, I better go now, I want to make love to you very much when you are sure it is right."

"My love, I am sure, I want you, I want to feel your body against me, I want you inside me, I do not want to wait any longer, come, hurry."

Her apartment was on the fifth floor, in the elevator, he felt her breasts as she stroked his groin. Both were inflamed with wanton desire. They hurried along the corridor, she fumbled the key hastily, managed to open the door, as soon as they were inside and the door closed, they undressed each other quickly, both completely naked, her back pressed against a wall, he hoisted her up, she entwined her legs around his waist and pulled him against her as he entered her. She uttered, "Yes, yes, I feel your wonderful cock." He rammed her, she responded, every time he pushed hard into her, she pushed forward, her hands were clutching his buttocks so fiercely that her fingernails dug into his flesh. It was raw, almost brutal sex that neither could have stopped even if they wanted to.

Maria had orgasmed and continued to do so, she shouted, "Harder, harder, fuck me harder, I won't break."

The crude words spurred him and he pounded her until he felt the tenseness, "I have to withdraw, I am going to come."

She tightened her legs as much as possible, "No, I want to feel you come, shoot your seed deep inside me." Her body was quivering, her eyes wide, her mouth open, panting as she felt him shudder and spurt his sperm, he jerked several times emptying his secretions. They held each other tight, his cock softened and slipped out. They slid down and lay on the floor, Maria on top of his body, both still panting a bit from their exertions.

He said, "Darling, you know I did not use a condom?"

"Yes, I will get some pills in the morning, I never want you to wear a condom, my love, were you shocked when I spoke rudely?"

"Honestly, no! People even at the top level of society use crude words and it turned me on even more. Making love to you was sensational, I hope you were satisfied."

She kissed him passionately and replied, "It was magic, I come many times."

She asked him, "Will you stay with me tonight, sleep with me, I will cook breakfast for us?"

"Maria, my wonderful, darling lady, a herd of wild horses could not drag me away from you, I want to hold you all night long."

She stared at him, a tear glistened in the corner of an eye, "John, I am madly in love with you."

He smiled at her, "And I am crazy about you, I love you, I just want to spend the rest of my life with you, to cherish you, to love you."

"Is that a proposal?" and she laughed.

"Maria, darling, you can take it as such or do you want me on bended knees facing your naked navel which would make me hot and bothered and give me a hard on as I ask you formally, my condition would make me stumble over the words."

She giggled and he laughed. "John, I am the happiest woman in the world, can we marry as soon as possible, I want to have children."

He replied, "Once the assignment is finished, I want to meet your father and formally ask him for your hand in marriage, any time after that we will marry. I will agree with everything you want; I am not a religious person but I will marry you in whatever ceremony makes you happy. Make all the arrangements, I will pay for everything, invite who you wish, I have only one person to invite, a person who I have disagreed with many times, my boss, but I am eternally grateful to him because of this assignment, otherwise I would never have met you. Oh, I forgot, there is a Spanish friend, he and his family will be invited. My father is a proud man, he will insist on paying."

"Try to dissuade him, I can pay, I am being well paid for this assignment and have enough money to live on for quite a while, whilst I seek another job."

"John, I will never insist or order you, if you want to remain in this organisation, I will accept the risks, I will worry of course when you are on an assignment but hopefully, we will have children which will keep me busy."

He looked at her, "Maria, you really are a special, fantastic woman. I will think about it. I imagine you will want to live in Spain, I will buy a nice property here, I will keep the lodge in Scotland, we can visit there for vacations at least twice a year. You know I quite fancy owning a ranch, a good sized one in good condition with stables, I would like to breed horses, have dogs and cats, I love animals, it would be a great place to raise kids."

Maria kissed him and held him tight, "Darling, that would be heaven, I love horses, I can ride horses very well and having dogs and cats would be great too."

"That is settled, we will start looking for a good property soon. Now we shower and go to bed."

She gave him a sly look, "We sleep or we do something else?"

"First, we make love, after, we sleep."

She stood up, took his hand and helped him to stand, "Come, we shower quickly." She gave him a mischievous smile and said, "Then you fuck me hard," and then laughed. In the shower, they sponged each other, spending most of the time sponging their most intimate parts which resulted in a certain physical reaction in him, she laughed and giggled when she saw it. They towelled each other dry and hurried to the bedroom. There they made love, less frantic than their first very physical coupling but still very passionate. They fell asleep entangled in each other's arms and legs.

The Fourth Day

John woke up, he was alone, he heard noises which he assumed was Maria bustling about. He got up, put on his boxers and padded into the small open kitchen. Maria had on a knee-length, belted terry towelling robe, she looked fantastic, no makeup, she had a freshly scrubbed look on her lovely face. She saw him and sidled into his embrace, they kissed, she said, "Sit down, breakfast will be ready soon." She served a huge omelette with pieces of bacon and mushrooms cut up in it. Coffee was poured, toast, butter and marmalade on the breakfast bar. They sat side by side, very close, at the bar. Both were famished and ate with gusto; she toasted more bread slices.

As they drank their third cup of coffee, he said, "I enjoyed that very much, I was starving."

She smiled, "All that wonderful exercise we did is good for an appetite, yes?"

He grinned, "The best exercise there is but I needed food for energy."

"I make sure you have plenty of energy," she laughed. "I will certainly need it, my love. What do you do today, John?"

"Not much, I am waiting on information, then I will be busy, I have a meeting at midday, it will last about 30 minutes then the rest of the day I am free, this morning we can have a walk, have churros and coffee somewhere on the Paseo."

"Okay we do that, after your meeting is finished would you like to go and meet my Mama and Papa, I have a small car, I can pick you up?"

"Yes, I want to meet your parents."

"Good, I will call them." She came and sat on his lap, her arms around his neck, the belt on her housecoat had come loose showing she was naked underneath. She felt his reaction and laughed.

"You are so sexy; I feel like ravishing you all the time."

She bit his ear and whispered, "I want you to ravish me now, I will say naughty words as you fuck me."

That did it, he picked her up and flung her on the unmade bed and went to work. An hour later, sated with their passion, they showered, dressed and went out. They sauntered hand in hand engrossed with each other, they had hot chocolate to dip their churros in, they chatted non-stop about the future. She went into a pharmacy whilst he remained outside. She flourished a small plastic bag, " I have a month's supply."

He laughed and remarked "Great, I hate using condoms." They walked back to her apartment block; he did not enter but left for his meeting with Diego.

The Meeting

Diego was already in the bar at the same table, instead of coffee, John ordered a bottle of Cruzcampo and Diego joined him drinking the same cerveza. "Mal, there is a strong buzz that something will happen tonight."

"You think there is a drug run tonight?"

"Yes, I feel for sure, I don't know where the landing or landings will be though."

"That's not a problem as long as the drugs are loaded and are on their way to Calais. I suggest that we do a continuous patrol tonight, I ride to and fro between two of the warehouse locales and you do the same with two other locales. We only have to see one vehicle on the move to confirm that there will be others. I will phone my boss then, that will give him plenty of time to organise everything in England. What time should we start our patrols?"

"The runs take place when there is still much traffic on the roads, I heard about 8 p.m."

"Okay, we start our patrols at 7 p.m., is that okay with you?"

"Yes, Mal, I hear more and more whispers that the chief of the Marbella town police is dirty. O'Reilly pays him monthly; I cannot confirm but I hear the sum is 5,000 euros a month."

"When I deal with O'Reilly, I will search for evidence, I am sure there will be detailed accounts in the villa and who receives bribes. Some wonderful personal news for you, when this operation has been tied up and finished I will be getting married, I have met the lady of my dreams here, we are quite simply madly in love. The wedding will take place, probably in Malaga, I want you, your wife and children to attend the wedding ceremony and reception."

Diego's face flushed with pleasure, "I would be honoured to attend, I am so happy for you."

"There is more, our plans are to buy a very nice ranch, to breed horses and raise a family somewhere in the area, if you hear of someplace up for sale, let me know."

"Mal, that is fantastic, I ride when I can, my family and I can visit you."

"I would like that very much, my name is not Mal, my real name is John, John Knox but keep it to yourself."

"I will, John, I cannot get over such wonderful news, can I tell Dulcena about the wedding?"

"Of course," Diego said, "we must drink more cerveza for your wonderful future." More beers were ordered and a variety of tapas. Diego toasted John who checked the time,

"Amigo, I have to go; I am going to Malaga with Maria to meet her parents."

"You will have no problem;, they will see that you are a great hombre."

John left and was walking back to Maria's, when a Renault Clio stopped alongside him, the front passenger door swung open and a familiar voice said, "Come on, get in, my love." He obeyed, Maria looked stunning, a tank top with thin straps, a knee-length skirt which had risen halfway up her thighs, her hair in a ponytail tied with a white bow, her face made up with light cosmetics, a pink lipstick had been applied and blue eyeshadow.

He said, "You look fabulous, Maria, I swear you look sexier and more beautiful every time I see you."

She laughed, "John, later, you can have your way with me, do anything you want but now we go to see my Mama and Papa, they want to meet you very much, they are excited that I have met a wonderful man and they are probably making plans for the wedding now. I have to be back at 5, I start work at 6."

"So no hanky panky today?"

"Hanky panky, what is that?" Then she laughed, "I know, no making love today."

He gave a broad smile, "That gives me time to build up a lot of energy."

She roared with laughter, "My darling, you will need lots of energy, so eat, rest and think of me."

The Parents

The drive to Malaga took less than an hour. Maria's parents had an apartment overlooking the beach, on the South side some distance from the port. She parked in the apartment car park, an uncovered park, not an underground one. They took the lift to the sixth floor. Before Maria pressed the doorbell, the door opened wide and her parents came forward, faces wreathed in smiles, they hugged and kissed Maria then both parents hugged John. Her mother was either late 50s or early 60s, she was a handsome woman, still slim, hair streaked with grey, John reckoned she must have been a great beauty when young. There was a strong resemblance between mother and daughter. The father was of the same age range, distinguished looking, well groomed, grey hair, moustache and a small beard.

Maria introduced John, both parents spoke excellent English, greeting him. John answered in fluent Castilan and asked them whether they preferred he speak Andalusian or Castilan or English as he complimented them on their English. Both parents were taken aback as their expressions showed. Then both chuckled, the father spoke to Maria in English, "Where did you find this remarkable man?" He turned to John, "I have never met anyone like you, your accents are perfect."

"Please forgive me for showing off, I wished to impress you and your beautiful lady."

"John, you succeeded, please call me Ramon and my lovely wife is called Rosita. Come have a drink and eat."

The sitting room/lounge was large, very nicely fashioned in a modern style, light and airy. At one end there was a long dining table that could seat ten persons next to an open hatch which give access to a large kitchen. On the table were wine glasses and beer glasses, a bottle of Rioja red wine had been uncorked, there was a large plate of slices of Serrano ham, another large plate of slices of Manchego mature cheese, a large plate of peeled prawns. "John, come and sit, would you like wine or beer or something stronger."

"Wine is perfect." The wine was poured, Maria asked him what he would like to eat, he replied, "I love every food on the table." She took a plate and filled it with ham, cheese and prawns and several breadsticks.

Rosita opened the conversation, "When Maria telephoned today, Ramon and I were very surprised, this is very sudden, we wondered what kind of man you were, it was what you say 'a bolt from the blue'."

"Rosita, Ramon, I met Maria a few days ago, yes, it is sudden I was attracted to Maria the second I saw and spoke to her and our relationship developed very fast. Maria and I have talked about many things, I am several years older, I want to marry Maria as soon as possible so Ramon I formally request Maria's hand in marriage. You must have a multitude of questions you wish to ask me, I tell you this, I love Maria with every fibre of my body, for me she is the most wonderful person in the world.

"Who and what am I and why am I here in Spain? Well, at the moment, I cannot fully answer, I am here on an assignment or mission I suppose one could call it. I work undercover, I hope to complete my task soon, when I succeed and I will, the world media will show reports all day and for some considerable time. I did intend to resign from my position but Maria is not sure I should, however we want to marry soon, I own an old house in Scotland which has been renovated and modernised, it is in a beautiful area, we will use it for vacations.

I intend to purchase a very suitable, nice ranch somewhere in this area, with stables and many acres of ground, I wish to have horses, to breed them, it will be a perfect environment to raise a family, we do want to have children That is a very brief summary,

Maria can tell you of my earlier background. Do you have any questions?"

Ramon replied, "You are a very direct and determined man, I respect that, Rosita also I am sure has the same opinion. We wondered and have been concerned about Maria for quite some time, there were no signs of her getting wed and we wondered if she ever would and whether we would ever have the joy of being grandparents, now suddenly so much has happened in a few days." Rosita gave a tiny nod, Ramon continued, "John, in the short time since we met, I have tried to read your character, you are very intelligent, strong mentally and physically, there is much we will never know, about your profession for instance but in our opinion, Maria could never wish for a finer man," and he gave John a broad smile, "John I am so happy to give you permission to marry Maria. She is a strong-minded daughter and regardless of my decision and opinion, she would have gone ahead and married you, come hell or high water."

Everyone broke into laughter, more wine was poured, Maria kissed her parents, brimming with happiness, Rosita and Maria's eyes showing tears of joy. Maria caught John's look and he felt the radiance of her love.

A discussion was held about the wedding plans; it was decided to fix a date after John had completed his assignment, there was a slight dispute between Ramon and John as to who would pay the costs of the wedding, a compromise was reached, they would split the costs 50 -50. Maria said, "Mama, Papa, we have to go now, I am working tonight, John and I will come back soon, there is much to talk about." Her parents hugged her and John, big smiles showing.

John said, "Thank you so much, I am looking forward to being a member of your wonderful family, adios for now."

In the car, Maria leaned over and kissed him, "My darling, you were wonderful, Mama and Papa were so impressed and they like you very much."

"They are great, I like them too." On the journey back, he told her that he would be on enquiries later, possibly for hours. She said, "I am off at 6 a.m. I will give you a keycard for the apartment, you can sleep there and I will see you in the morning."

He grinned, "Will you give me a wake-up-call?"

Her eyes twinkled, "What do you think, my darling?"

"The same as you, the thoughts are having an effect on me." She checked the time and giggled, "We have time for a quickie what you Brits call it." She accelerated, "Take it easy, let's get there safely." She laughed out loud and slowed down a little.

When they arrived, as soon as the door was shut, they made love standing up only partially undressed, her skirt was above her waist, her panties crotch pulled to the side as he entered her. The coupling was short, both of them climaxed, Maria was gasping, "My darling, I love you, you make me hot, I feel on fire when you fuck me."

He laughed. "Maybe you just love my cock."

"You beast, I love you," and then she laughed. "Yes, I love your cock as well." She got ready for her work, showered and changed her attire. She gave him a keycard. They walked to the hotel, he went to his room and changed, donning his all black outfit. He went down in the elevator to the basement vehicle park. He received a call from Diego to confirm the locations they were patrolling, then he set off.

Night Movements

John patrolled the main road between the two side turnings he knew, Diego was patrolling further along the Carretera. At about 8.45, two motorcyclists with pillion passengers passed him travelling quite fast but within the speed limit. He saw them turn into side road leading to the first warehouse, he phoned Diego, he informed him and asked, "Anything happening in your area.?"

"Nothing so far, wait I see two motorcyclists with passengers, they have turned off and onto the road that leads to a warehouse."

"Diego, this is it, these guys are probably the truck drivers, find a spot and park up, there should be some type of vehicles coming soon, try and video their details, I will be doing the same."

About an hour later, John saw three pickup types of vehicles with covers over the rear carrying part, he recorded them, each vehicle had at least three occupants, all were different makes and models, different colours too. Forty minutes later, four large vehicles emerged from the side road and turned left to go north. Two were articulated HGVs (heavy goods vehicles); the other two were pantechnicons, boxed in type vehicles As they passed, John managed to record most of the details with his smartphone.

Fifteen minutes later, Diego reported similar movements which he had recorded. "Great work, let's go to the bar and have a few drinks." John was the first to arrive, he ordered tapas plus a plate of Boquerón's and a plate of French fries. Diego came in, the bottles of beer were on the table. "I'm thirsty and hungry," he remarked. They got stuck into the food which was consumed in a very short time, more beers were ordered, John asked him, "Send everything you recorded to my phone now, I will forward the lot to my boss, now we wait and hopefully receive good results from England. We can relax for a couple of days."

"After the results, what then?"

"Not sure, I think I will deal with Brown first and then it will be O'Brien. Diego who is the top Guardia Civil guy and is he straight, not on the take?"

"General Juan Ferandez, his office is in Malaga, he is a tough hombre, it has been said he does not like foreigners but he does have friends in Britain."

"That's too bad, after I have dealt with O'Reilly I will visit him and tell him a few things."

"We have to bring in the Spanish authorities to deal with all the people in the pickups, after I have spoken to the general, I assure you he will cooperate." Diego noted the serious expression on John's face and thought, *the General is in for a rough ride.*

After one more Cruzcampo each, they called it a night. "As soon as I receive reports from England, I will call you, thank you for your assistance, amigo." John went to the hotel and spoke to Maria, "I am just changing my clothes here, I will be going to the apartment soon."

She murmured, "Make sure you have no clothes on when I get home," and she licked her lips and gave a sexy smile.

"Madam Sergeant Major, I assure you everything will be standing to attention." She laughed gleefully as he left the desk. In his room. He undressed, showered, changed into fresh clothes and called Huntsman.

He passed the information and sent the videos. Huntsman was quite frankly, ecstatic and excited. "All will be set in motion, someone will be sent to Calais to observe the customs and what action, if any, is taken. I never envisaged any results this early, this will stir things in the corridors of power."

"It's not over until O'Reilly and his bunch have been dealt with and I will execute that task when I receive news from you, I want to have the pleasure of informing him that his organisation in England has been destroyed."

"Please don't take risks, your life is worth more than all the evil scum on this earth." John was taken aback by this and he thought, *the old bugger sounds seriously worried about me.*

He said, "Don't worry, I don't intend to, I have too much to live for without taking any stupid chances." The call ended and Huntsman pondered about John's last comment. He could only surmise that John had met someone whom he cared for.

John left the hotel; Maria was dealing with someone so he winked as he passed reception. He walked to the apartment stopping at a cafe on the way and had a Cafe con leche. He was not tired; his mind was filled with so many thoughts, Maria, her parents, Huntsman, tonight's events, the future and what would he do, he would have to have a regular income to maintain a family. He could get a teaching position or write novels or non-fiction travel books. He was quite well off, he had invested in excellent companies, he had three bank accounts, he had been frugal and with the salary for the assignment he reckoned he would have over 2,000,000 pounds not counting the lodge. He ordered a Spanish brandy, a double and just sat watching the passers-by. He stayed there for another 40 minutes and then went to the apartment.

The Fifth Day

John was fast asleep when Maria came. She showered, towelled herself dry and then applied dabs of perfume on parts of her body, went to bed and slid in against John, spoon fashion. She felt really horny, she wanted to be loved so she set to work on John stroking him very gently, it had the desired effect, he became rock hard, at the same time she tongued and nibbled his ears. He woke up, felt her stroking and said, "You sexy minx, alright I will give you what you want." He turned round to face her and manoeuvred her on her back with him on top, he gripped her wrists and held them apart above her head and then penetrated her making her gasp with the sudden intrusion of his cock. He was rampant as he rode her making her moan and utter sounds of delight.

"Yes, yes, my darling, I want you so much, oh, oh, I come now, are you coming my love?"

He grunted, "Now," and he spurted inside of her. He lay at the side of her, her head snuggled against his neck.

"John, I love you, the feelings I have for you are incredible, I never realised what real love and sex was, you have wakened all these emotions in me."

He kissed her gently on her eyes, "My darling, words are inadequate to describe my love for you, I am the most content and happiest man in the world all because of you." They cuddled each other blissfully in each other's arms for some time and Maria fell asleep. John, very slowly moved from her embrace and got out of bed. He moved quietly, had a shower and dressed. He had breakfast, three boiled eggs, toast and coffee.

He sat outside on the terrace and observed the activities on the paseo, joggers, people walking dogs, skate boarders, couples arm in arm, it was a beautiful sunny day. Maria woke up about 12.30, she put on her housecoat, entered the lounge, saw John on the terrace, she approached quietly and placed her arms around his neck and kissed his head. She said, "I am hungry."

"For food or for me?"

"For both."

"Get dressed, I'll take you out for lunch." He rose up and turned her around and playfully gave her a slight slap on her shapely bottom. "Go and get ready."

She laughed and said "Beast," stuck her tongue out at him and scampered when he moved towards her.

They had lunch at one of the fish restaurants next to the beach. A simple meal of grilled sardines, bread and white wine. After, they had a walk along the paseo, engrossed in each other, oblivious to everything else. They had ice cream cones. She said, "I have never been so happy, I love you my wonderful, darling John."

"My love, then you know how I feel, I am the luckiest man in the world."

"John, we go back now and go to bed?"

"Yes."

They returned to the apartment and spent the time in bed making love until Maria had to rise and get ready for work. "Darling, what are you doing tonight?"

"I'll go out for a meal, have a couple of beers, come back and watch TV. I'll probably have an early night, tomorrow I am expecting news from England so tomorrow night I will be busy." She did not ask him what he would be doing but just told him she would see him in the morning. When she was ready he said, "I'll walk you to the hotel, I want to visit my room." They walked hand in hand until they neared the hotel and then disengaged. He went to his room; he had a feeling that matters could accelerate so he strapped the knife on just above the ankle. Checked the handgun with the suppressor attached, stuck it inside his waist belt in the small of his back and slipped two magazines in his trouser pockets, he put on a lightweight jacket which hid the gun. He left the room; he handed the keycard to Maria.

He murmured, "See you in the morning." She nodded; the other receptionist was only a few feet away attending to a guest. It was not policy for a staff member to be having an affair with a guest, so for now Maria had to be discreet.

A Sea Trip

John had a walk about the main thoroughfare and went to an Italian restaurant. He had a medium-sized pepperoni pizza, two glasses of Chianti and coffee. He had just finished the meal and was about to pay the bill when his phone rang, "John, where are you?" It was Diego. "At the Tuscany restaurant."

"I'll be there to pick you up in a minute."

He settled the bill, stepped outside as Diego came. He got on the motorcycle and they sped off. "John, a short time ago at the villa, Brown and four men got into a car, they had placed what looked like a body into the boot of the car, it was wrapped in a black type of cloth. I am sure they are going to the port to take the boat out to sea, we have to get there."

"Drop me off as close as possible as long as the car hasn't reached there yet, I have to get on the boat, can you hire or borrow a motor launch, I want you to follow the boat but at several 100 metres distance, when and if it stops, keep well aware, at least 300 to 400 metres."

"Okay, the boat is the Wild Rover, what's your plan?"

"A bit sketchy at the moment, I suspect the body is O'Brien's wife, whether it is or not does not alter things, this is my chance to deal with Brown."

"You are outnumbered, will you be okay?"

"My friend, it is not quantity that counts but quality." He gave a huge grin, They arrived at the port, Diego cruised slowly along the quayside. "The car is not here, the boat is moored over there, quick go now, I know where to get a launch."

The Wild Rover was a big yacht, at least 60 feet in length, very sleek, two jet skis and an outboard rubber dinghy were lashed down on the stern deck which was next to the quay, a gangway was in place with a chain strung across the access gap to the boat. John glanced around to see if anybody was watching, there were a few people in the vicinity but no one was paying attention to him. He quickly got on board and looked for cover, he gained entry to the interior, it was luxuriously fitted out, with a large lounge, there was a stairway leading to the lower deck, he went down and found there were four fair sized cabins, all with double beds, en suite showers and built in wardrobes. He looked around rapidly, found an empty wardrobe and hid in it.

About five minutes later, he heard the movement of several people, they were talking but he could not discern the words. A few minutes passed and then the engine started, a very powerful loud sound. The boat then began to move from its berth very slowly. When it left the port, it gained speed. He remained in hiding. After a time, about 20 to 30 minutes, he estimated the craft slowed down and the engine was stopped, it was a calm sea and the craft gently swayed to and fro. John left the cabin, gun in his hand, the safety off. He crept up the staircase, at the top he glanced around. He heard voices from the stern. He moved silently the five men were standing around a figure on the deck, two of them were attaching chains and weights. They were absorbed they did not hear him, three had their backs to him the other two were the ones fixing the weights.

"Well, well, what do we have here, the Boston tea party? Oh, I see not tea but a body." All five were startled and they all faced him. "Line up the other side of the body."

Brown sneered and replied, "There are five of us, are you going to shoot us all with that peashooter?" John fired once, a hole appeared in the middle of a forehead, blood showed and the man collapsed.

"Now there are four, who wants to be next." They gazed in horror and astonishment.

"I have questions, I want answers, not bullshit, let me see who that is, uncover the face? Do it now." The three men looked at Brown who nodded. One bent down and uncovered the top half of the body. It was Sue, naked and with bruising around her neck.

John felt a coldness, an icy rage. "She has been strangled, who did it?" Silence, John fired a second shot, same result, a bullet in the centre of the forehead. "Who wants to be number three, once more, who killed her?"

Brown replied, "Who do you think, her loving husband of course."

"O'Reilly murdered her?"

"I just said that."

"A few months ago, two men were brought on board, who killed them?" Silence, he raised the gun and one of them blurted out, "He did," and pointed at Brown.

"For what reason?" Silence, John fired and shattered Brown's right kneecap, he pointed the weapon at the left kneecap. Brown had roared with pain, "Because they were snooping, asking questions."

"How did they die, you interrogated them no doubt and tortured them?"

"Of course, I fucking did, I made the fuckers suffer."

"Really, what method did you use?"

Brown laughed, "I used a fucking knife and cut strips off them now put a bullet in me, you're going to kill me anyway and these two fucking wimps held them down, laughing as I did it. They were still alive when they were thrown overboard and I fucking enjoyed it." John fired three times, Brown's left kneecap was shattered and the other two men were shot in their foreheads. "The two men you tortured were my colleagues, they were only doing their job. You will die but it will be an excruciating painful death." Brown was lying on the deck in agony, John fired twice, shattering both of Brown's elbows. Brown howled in agony, "Who the fuck are you?"

"I'm the poofter that was at O'Reilly's sex party."

Brown said, "If I tell you a few things, will you finish me off with a bullet in the head?"

"I promise you a quick death if what you tell me is good information."

"O'Reilly has a safe room, you slide a large cupboard in the kitchen to one side, there are steps to a cellar, in there he has a large safe where he keeps all the important stuff, he has another safe in his bedroom just for show, not much in it. There are hidden cameras in all the bedrooms, he takes movies of everyone fucking, couples, threesomes, arsehole bandits, he has the black on a lot of important people, coppers, politicians, TV and film people. British, Spanish and others.

"Why are you telling me this, apart from wanting a quick death?"

"Because the fucker has the black on me, he has proof that I offed a couple years ago back in the smoke. You're no poofter, you are the hardest fucker I've ever come across." He squinted at John, "You've got a stake in this and it's not the two snoopers."

John nodded towards Sue's body. "Several years ago I was in love with Sue, we broke up, well I broke the relationship because of the work I did, I took this job because of the gen that O'Reilly was going to get rid of her, his third wife, he was suspected of killing his first two wives."

Brown said, "He killed them, he killed one with a huge overdose, the other he strangled and dumped her at sea, Mister whoever you are, believe me I never laid a finger on any woman, O'Reilly got your lady on drugs, he made her a junkie, she was a real beauty once and I liked her. You think I'm a real bastard, well, O'Reilly is the most evil fucker there is, fucking cunning so watch out when you go after him, I am sorry about her, she didn't deserve that, I hope the fucker burns in hell."

John stared at him and thought Brown was a brutal man but he did have a tiny spark of morality inside that hulk and was seeking redemption. John said, "Thank you," pressed the muzzle against Brown's forehead and fired. He then picked Sue up and took her to a cabin, placed her on a bed and covered her nakedness up to her neck. He kissed her on the forehead. "Rest in peace, Sue." He then got to work, he found two containers of fuel which he splashed about in the lounge and on the outside decks. He looked for and found a very pistol, stuffed cartridges in his pockets. He managed to heave the dinghy overboard and tied it to a railing. He got into the dinghy and tested the outboard motor; it fired after three attempts. He climbed back on board the yacht and looked for the galley, in it was a stove fuelled by propane gas, he turned the tank on and turned on all the stove switches to full. He then returned and clambered into the dinghy, untied it, as it drifted away he started the engine. He steered it away for about 100 metres, stern towards the yacht, he then fired the very pistol several times, he saw the flicker of flames so he sped away as fast as possible, he was about 300 metres away when there was an explosion, then another, the yacht was ablaze, burning from prow to stern. He kept moving fast until he saw Diego waving from a launch. Diego pulled him aboard, John used his knife to make several holes and slashes in the dinghy which sank quickly, the engine weight dragging it under. He dropped the very pistol and cartridges into the sea.

Diego could see a sombre expression on John's face, "Are you okay. Amigo, are you injured?"

"No, I am fine, the body was O'Reilly's wife, he strangled her. Brown redeemed himself, I guess, he gave me a lot of information. I will wait for news from my boss and then I will deal with him, Brown and the other four are dead." Diego thought that John must be one of the deadliest men ever. John was quiet all the way back to the port, the blazing boat could be seen all the way back, they managed to ease into the marina and into a berth. Minutes later, they were on the quay heading to where Diego parked the motorcycle. There were many onlookers on the quay. All looking and pointing to the blazing boat, suddenly the blaze was quenched as the yacht slid under the surface.

"Diego, I need a drink and something to eat, stop at our usual bar."

"Okay, amigo, I want a drink too." They arrived at the bar, excited noisy conversations between the patrons were taking place. The subject-the burning craft.

John gave a little smile. "News travels fast, O'Reilly will see or hear about it, he won't know for sure whether it was his until Brown and the others don't show up, then his mind will go into overdrive."

"Will he not leave, run away?"

"No, he will stay, he has no alternative, where would he go, it takes time to make proper arrangements, he will claim insurance for the craft, he will say it was stolen by drug runners, he will not move out of the villa."

"How much would the ship be worth?"

"I do not know, quite a few million I guess." Tapas were ordered and pints of draught Cruzcampo were consumed in record time. More tapas and pints were ordered. John was more relaxed now, tired but satisfied with the events. "Diego, how deep is it where the yacht went down?"

"I think over 200 metres."

"Too deep for scuba divers on compressed air, they will need specialised diving suits and equipment to check the wreck."

"John, they might not bother, the expense could be too much."

"It's been quite a night, I'm going now, I hope to get a report from my boss tomorrow night, let's have our usual meeting okay?"

"Sure, okay." John settled the bill and left. Diego remained and had a coffee, thinking about the night's events and John in particular, he wondered what made a man like John, what was his background, his history, he had never met anyone like him, lethal, loving, polite, quite complex, a man who inspired loyalty and trust. He finished his coffee, paid and went to his lodgings.

John went to the hotel to leave his weapons in the room safe. He did not want to have them at Maria's apartment. She was dealing with a guest when he passed by, their eyes met as he walked past. In the room, he showered, changed into fresh clothes, put the weapons into the safe and went down to reception. Maria was alone, he went to the desk, "I'm going to the apartment now, see you in the morning, Darling."

She replied, "You look tired."

"I am a bit tired; a good night's sleep and I will be ready for anything in the morning." He smiled as he spoke.

"Anything?" She said.

He grinned. "Definitely." He lowered his tone, "I want to ravish you, my love, make you scream with passion."

"You beast, you're making me hot." He laughed and walked off. She watched him as he left following his movements with adoring eyes. When he entered the apartment, he phoned the boss and told him about the night's event, he missed nothing out except for the information given by Brown. There was silence for several moments and then, "I am deeply sorry about Susan, you have done an amazing job. You have rid the world of these inhuman monsters. Well done."

The Villa

O'Reilly was alone, pacing back and forward, shouting into his cell phone, "You're a fucking copper and you don't know shit, my boat is missing, where the fuck is it? Is it the one that was on fire? I want to know what happened to the crew. Get back to me soon, earn your fucking money." He threw the phone onto a settee, he kept pacing and thinking. He was certain the yacht had been sunk but where were Brown and the others, did they manage to get rid of Susan? Not knowing was sending him crazy, he was frantic. How did the yacht catch fire, was it accidental or not? If it wasn't an accident, it meant there was someone out there working against him, if so, who was it? It was certainly not a rival gang boss involved in the drugs business; he would have known about that. Could it be the law? He was not sure; he would have been told by his police contacts if that was the case.

Tanya had gone to bed but when she heard him shouting, she came downstairs dressed in a negligee that showed off her body. She went to him and put her arms around his neck, "Damien, baby, come to bed."

"I can't, I have to know what happened, make yourself useful, make a pot of coffee, no bed for me until I know what the fucks going on."

"I stay, give you a massage, suck your cock, fuck you, anything, make you relax."

"Just make the fucking coffee then fuck off back to bed." She pouted and went to the kitchen, made the coffee, left it on a coffee table, and then flounced off back to bed. O'Reilly continued his pacing.

The Sixth Day

John was still fast asleep when Maria came home. She showered, dried herself and slid in against him. He woke up in seconds when he felt her body pressed tight against his back whilst her hands and lips were busy. He uttered, "You sexy witch."

She just laughed and said, "Did I wake you, my love?" He grinned.

"Yes, in the best way possible." They made love, stayed in bed, and both fell asleep.

His phone rang, it was after 10 a.m. "The convoy arrived at Calais, 12 vehicles, they were not even given a cursory check. Their progress is being monitored; each one will be observed all the way to their destinations, CCTV, motorway patrols, personnel from various units are all involved, every police force is standing by, at the moment we do not know their ultimate destinations but when they arrive they will be detained and kept under wraps until every vehicle and crew is in custody. I will update you until all the vehicles have been seized."

John said, "Thanks." Maria awoke.

"Who was that, darling?"

"My boss."

"What did he want?"

"It was a progress report, I will tell you about it later, now that I am wide awake, I will have my evil way and then we get ready to go out and eat somewhere." She threw the sheets off and lay naked legs apart. "Do it, fuck me." He obliged for the next 30 minutes, then they showered. They had a late breakfast at an English restaurant, he checked the time, "I have the usual meeting shortly, I can walk you home or you can come with me and meet Diego?"

"I come with you."

Just after 12 noon, they entered the bar where Diego was at the usual table, he stood up as they came to the table. "Diego, this is Maria."

Diego took her left hand, raised it and kissed it saying, "Maria, you are so beautiful, I am honoured to meet you. John is one very lucky man, please sit, what would you like to drink?"

"Wine gracias." The three of them chatted away about the wedding.

Maria said, "I want to meet your wife and children, can I visit them?"

"Of course, Dulcena would love to meet you. John has mentioned his plans about a ranch, that is wonderful."

"Yes, it is a dream come true, We are very happy, you and your family will visit us many times, yes?"

"Yes."

John mentioned to Diego, "All is working to plan, I am going to get further reports today. Now, I am going to take Maria to a jeweller, I will contact you later." Diego paid the bill.

When John and Maria were outside she said, "You did not say anything about a jeweller before.!"

"My darling, I want to show the world that you are engaged to be married. I will buy you a ring, I want you to choose a good one, expense is no object, it is an expression of the love I feel for you."

She peered at him, tears forming at the corners of her eyes, "My darling, I love you, I accept your offer, thank you, thank you."

They visited two jewellers before she chose a ring, she was hesitant when she saw the price tag, he saw her reaction, "Do you like it?"

"Yes."

"That is all that matters, try it on, it might need some adjustment or they may have different sizes of the same model." The shop assistant confirmed that they had two more rings of the same design. One fitted perfectly. The design was a three-carat diamond, surrounded by sapphires in a circular shape The rest of the ring was platinum. John had two Visa credit cards, one in his own name and one in the assumed name of McColl. He used the one in his own name. Maria kept the ring on her finger and kept looking at it. As soon as they left the shop, she hugged and kissed him, tears in her eyes. "Thank you, my wonderful lovely man, once again you have made the day perfect." She then chortled with delight, "The other receptionists will get a surprise when I wave my hand about."

On the way to the apartment, they had a celebratory drink outside on the terrace of the bar. She remembered his comment to Diego. "John, what did you mean when you spoke to Diego that all is working to plan?"

He smiled, "By tomorrow I should be able to explain but not now, okay?"

"Okay, what are you doing tonight.?"

"Maria, you are a curious lady, you know the saying *curiosity killed the cat*?"

"Cats also have nine lives, they purr, like cream and have sharp claws, I purr when we make love, I like cream and I can use my claws."

"Yeah, I felt your claws sticking in my buttocks."

She let out a loud laugh, "I can do it again."

The time was 4.45 p.m. She said, "We go home now, I have to get ready for work." They were back at the apartment before 5, she said, "I shower, shower with me." They both stripped and entered the shower where they made love, her back against the wall, her legs around his waist, she was vocal as usual, as she nibbled his neck she murmured in his ear, "Fuck me hard, I love your hard cock, harder, yes, yes, yes, oh, oh I come." Her body convulsed as he pumped his sperm into her, he kept ramming hard until he had emptied every drop. She laughed delightedly as he sat on the shower floor, she sat on his lap facing him, "John, you have made me so that I want you to fuck me all the time, I think maybe I become a nymphomaniac."

"Well, if there is a word for a male nymphomaniac then that is what I have become, I cannot resist you, I love you, every part of you, I love your personality, your character, sense of humour, your body, your voice."

"We were made for each other, yes?"

"Yes, a thousand times yes." She kissed him, had a quick grope then hastily moved before he could retaliate.

They dressed, she viewed her ring, "I want to show to everyone, you walk with me to the hotel?"

"Yes, I want to visit my room." They strolled hand in hand to the hotel. As they entered; members of staff stared at them as they were still holding hands. Maria flourished her left hand drawing attention to it; the receptionists whooped and ran to inspect her ring; they all started chattering like demented chickens. John went up to his room, retrieving the keycard himself. He collected the weapons. He dressed in black, strapping the knife to his right ankle. The girls were still chattering as he passed, Maria saw him and raised her eyebrows as if to say, 'What are you up to, what's happening?'

He phoned Diego, "Stand by, I will probably need your assistance tonight. Twelve vehicles entered England earlier today, I am expecting a call from my boss then I will go to O'Reilly's." He went to a bar, had a large slice of Spanish tortilla and coffee. He had two more Cafe con leches, his phone rang before 8 p.m.

"We have all the vehicles, the drivers and many more who were waiting to unload and distribute the drugs. There are countless interrogations going on, most of the captives are singing like canaries. There are squads of drug enforcement officers visiting many addresses now and it is expected that in all, there will be 100s of arrests. Everyone is flushed, excited, the vehicles are being dismantled; the packages being hidden in several different places. The final count of the packages is not yet known but early estimates of the street value is several hundred million. This is the biggest drug bust ever in the UK, possibly in the world; the final count may be around a billion pounds. The powers are over the moon. I have a high-level meeting tomorrow with many heads of organisations, the PM, the Home Secretary, all the security services, top police officers etc. are attending. This is all due to you, the short time involved, the results are beyond belief. Everyone attending the meeting will want to know how you succeeded in such a short time when all other agencies and organisations have failed over the years. I am elated and so proud of you."

"It's not over for me, I will visit O'Reilly tonight and deliver the news to him. I may have further good news for you, I know where he has a secret stash, a very large safe which he does not know that anyone else is aware of. I will finish the job; O'Reilly is a walking corpse but he does not know that. After I have finished this assignment, I am out of the organisation. I want a peaceful existence. I have met a wonderful lady, we are engaged to be married, we have made plans to reside in Spain, buy a ranch, breed horses and hopefully raise a family."

"I understand how you feel, I am so happy for you and your fiancé, she must be a very special person. I do not blame you for leaving. I will come to Spain in two days' time, I have much to tell you. You will be extremely interested in what I have to say, I would like to meet your lady and she should hear everything I have to tell you. Thank you for all that you have accomplished. Please be careful when you confront O'Reilly, he has killed so many."

"So have I, all of them, evil monsters like him." The call ended.

The Final Conflict

John rode the motorcycle at a leisurely pace; there was no urgency. As he neared the turning to enter the private road to the villa, he saw two men dressed in dark clothes wearing caps and sidearms in waist holsters. John parked and approached them, speaking Spanish he told them that he wished to see Senor O'Reilly. Both of them came up close to him, he could smell garlic on their breath. One said, "No, no one is allowed in, our boss is with Senor O'Reilly." It dawned on John that the chief police officer of Marbella was with O'Reilly.

He said, "Oh, the one who is on O'Reilly's payroll, does O'Reilly pay you two as well?" Angry expressions appeared.

The same one said, "Go away now, dangerous talk means bad trouble for you," his right hand moved towards the holster and then he unclipped it.

"Wrong move, old son." John jabbed fingers into the officer's eyes and pirouetted kicking high, striking the other officer under the jaw, breaking bone and teeth and causing the officer to bite his tongue, he then delivered a hard kick to the first one's groin causing intense pain and harm to the testicles. He then went to work on them really seriously, he fractured their wrists and ankles. He dragged them both to the side of the road, both in anguish, groaning and mumbling. He slapped their faces, "Listen very carefully, corrupt cops are the most despised scum I hate. I suggest you crawl and hide somewhere, if I find you here when I return, your next destination will be the morgue, do you understand, just nod if you do?" Both nodded, fear in their eyes. "One question, how many more men are at the villa, look at my hand, nod when I show the correct number." When he showed four fingers, both nodded.

He continued along the lane, parking the motorcycle about 100 metres from the front entrance. When he was about 30 metres from it, two guards met him, both dressed the same as the two he had dealt with, both had sidearms, one in his 40s, portly built, about 5 feet 8 inches tall, the other in his late 20s, slim built, over 6 feet tall. The elder one spoke in broken English, "How you get here, why you here?"

John replied in the Andalusian dialect, surprising both guards. "I came to see Senor Brown and your boss, the two guards are both injured, they cannot move, now I suggest you let me pass, that you leave here and go and help your comrades, summon an ambulance."

Both men stared, speechless for a few moments, trying to collect their thoughts and were indecisive. John said, "How many more guards are there, tell me quickly, my patience is vanishing?"

The elder one gulped and replied "Dos."

"Go and find them and bring them here, pronto." Both of them scuttled off and were back in a few minutes. The other two were both in their mid-30s, one had a grim, hard expression. He said, "Who are you to order us, we are four, you are only one."

John replied, "Do not try me, all of you are cops, right? I do not know what the police regulations are in Spain but I am certain the authorities will not approve of you guarding a criminal who is a murderer, an evil gang boss who is a big drug dealer. I know that in the villa the Chief Officer of Marbella police is having a meeting with O'Reilly, now all of you either fuck off or suffer the consequences."

There was a hurried discussion, three of them wanted to go; the hard-faced one was against them. John sighed, "So be it." He delivered a hard kick to the dissenter causing him to bend forward as he moaned in agony and clutched his groin region. John punched the side of his head rupturing an eardrum, he then grabbed the right arm in a rigid lock and brought it down hard over his thigh causing a fracture of the elbow. He did the same to the left arm. All of this happened in seconds, so fast, he pulled the guard towards him and then brought his knee up fast and hard, fracturing his jaw. The guard collapsed onto the ground in severe pain. John prodded him with his foot and said, "Who's next?" There were horrified, terrified looks from the other three, they had not moved a muscle. "Take this turd and pick up the other two, take them to a hospital emergency, now move." They scampered, supporting the injured guard and took him to a parked car, they helped him in it, strapped the seat belt on him, they were gone in a minute.

He entered the villa through the front door; he heard voices coming from the lounge. He crept to the lounge door which was ajar, he switched his smart phone recorder on and listened to a very heated argument. O'Reilly was doing most of the ranting, "You're head of the fucking police here and you know fuck all, you don't fucking know where Brown and the others are, you don't know what happened to my boat, what do you fucking know, why the fuck do I pay you?"

"Please, Senor, my men guard you all day and night, I have men investigating the sinking of your ship when I have answers, I tell you."

John peered through the narrow gap between the door and jamb, he could see an overweight uniformed town police officer, a man in his 50s, a swarthy complexion with a small pencil moustache, sitting in an armchair. O'Reilly was prowling back and forward like a caged ferocious animal. O'Reilly kept on shouting, "What the fuck do I pay you for?" Before the officer could answer, John heard a female voice speak English but with an accent, "Darling, come to bed, you no sleep for long time."

"Tanya, fuck off, I've got too much to think about.

John decided it was time to make an entrance, he gripped his handgun in his right hand, holding it behind him and he swung the door open, three pairs of eyes swivelled towards him. He said, "Can I join the party? It does seem a jolly little do." The officer made a grab for his handgun, John waited until it was clear of the holster then he fired, hitting the hand, causing the weapon to drop. "Naughty, naughty, try anything else and I will shoot your prick off." He said this in Spanish, the officer's eyes opened wide. His right arm drooping, the hand bleeding profusely.

O'Reilly said, "Who the fuck are you?"

"Your nemesis, in other words your worst nightmare." John spoke to Tanya who had a see through negligee on, "Go and put some clothes on, gather your belongings and get out of here, hurry, I'll give you ten minutes, no longer." She scurried away.

O'Reilly then said, "I know you, you were at the party, the fucking Jock heir to some bog estate, what the fuck are you doing here.?"

"Destroying your empire, have you seen the English or world news recently, switch the TV on, there is something of interest concerning you."

The TV was switched on; O'Reilly used the remote until he found an English news channel. A reporter was doing an outside broadcast, standing outside a garage, there were police officers, cars with flashing blue lights. "It is calculated that this is the biggest drug raid in world history, many similar actions are taking place all over England. 100s of arrests have been made, even now, more are expected." O'Reilly's face was pale with a sheen of perspiration. "You are finished. Police officers are on their way now to arrest you for a number of murders. For a start, your three wives, two of which you strangled, the other by injecting a drug overdose."

"Bollocks."

"Brown made a dying declaration; he really hated you; he was a brute but he despised you for killing and ill-treating women and you know that. You will end up in prison for life and I do mean life." O'Reilly was really sweating, trying to put some thoughts together. Tanya appeared carrying a suitcase and a large handbag, she hurried past them and left the room. John backed up, keeping his gun on O'Reilly and the officer then watched her go out the front door. He said, "Where's your shooter?"

"Fuck off." John pistol-whipped him across the bridge of his nose, breaking skin, causing blood to flow. "I repeat, where is your shooter?"

"In that drawer." He indicated to a table drawer. John watched the both of them carefully as he checked the drawer. There was a loaded.38 revolver in it. He took out a surgical glove from his pocket, slipped it on his left hand, lifted the revolver, spun the chamber to check it. He then shot the officer between the eyes. "That is one more murder on your plate and a Spanish senior police officer at that, my you are a bad boy."

O'Reilly's were wide open, his body started to shake, he could barely speak. "Fucking hell, you're fucking mad."

John grinned, "Not mad, just a pest controller, I exterminate rats. Let's have a look in your safe."

A crafty glint appeared in O'Reilly's eyes, "You want money, everyone has a price, how much?"

"More than you can pay, I am very expensive, show me the safe and no tricks. If I see any trace of a weapon, you are dead." Before they left the room, John picked up the officer's gun with his gloved hand and tucked it in his belt. He left O'Reilly's weapon on the floor next to the officer.

They went upstairs to a bedroom, O'Reilly moved a large oil painting, behind it was a wall safe. O'Reilly opened it and took out several wads of notes, euros, pounds, U.S. dollars, he said, "There are about 300,000 pounds in different currencies, it's yours, just let me walk away."

"Just peanuts, I told you not to try any tricks." He pistol-whipped him again on the same part. O'Reilly howled in agony. John placed the gun in O'Reilly's mouth, sweat pouring down his face, eyes wide open showing fear, O'Reilly was quivering in terror. "I said no tricks, now show me the safe in the cellar, where is your computer?"

"I don't have one of these fucking machines, they can be hacked, I don't trust them, what fucking safe?"

"One last chance, show me or die here and now, I can find it myself. I am merely trying to shorten matters, the entrance to the cellar is in the kitchen behind a cupboard, now move or die." O'Reilly was given a shove, they went to the kitchen where a large cupboard was moved out and towards the side, a head-high opening was revealed, a set of light switches on the wall. All were switched on, steps led down into the cellar. O'Reilly led, being prodded by John. The cellar was quite large, dominated by a huge safe, set into a wall, similar to the ones in bank vaults. There was a large type of wheel in the centre of the door. An electronic display with an inbuilt key system, showing numbers and letters was inset in the door. "Open it." O'Reilly looked despairingly at John who prodded O'Reilly's groin with the pistol. "Three seconds then I shoot your prick and balls off."

Hastily, O'Reilly entered a sequence of numbers and letters, filmed by John's smartphone. The wheel was spun to one side, when it clicked, it was spun the other way until it clicked again then it was pulled open. It was a walk-in type, massive interior, with drawers, small and large. "Lie flat, hands behind your head, do not move one muscle."

O'Reilly obeyed, he pleaded, "Take what you want, just let me walk away with a few quid."

"If it is worth it, I might do that."

John began looking at the contents, precious stones of every description, two necklaces he recognised as being famous, having been stolen, worth millions. Two Faberge eggs, platinum and gold ingots. Many wads of different currencies. Registers and account books, many documents giving details of offshore accounts in Liechtenstein, Channel Islands, Isle of Man, and the Cayman Islands. One large drawer was full of DVDs. In the registers were details of power boats, vehicles, names of distributors in the UK, the locations of drug processing laboratories in Morocco and Algeria. There were lists of phone numbers from many countries, the USA, Mexico, South America, Thailand, Myanmar, Laos, Afghanistan, the Philippines etc. John had hit the mother lode so to speak. There was a mass of information that would create so much work and initiate 1000s of investigations throughout the world.

He prodded O'Reilly, "Get up, back to the lounge where we can talk." In the lounge, he pushed him back in the same armchair opposite the corpse. John stood behind the corpse and using the officer's.38 revolver, shot O'Reilly on the nose thus covering the pistol whipping. He prised open the officer's right hand, the 9 mm bullet fortunately was in the hand, he used the tip of his knife to retrieve it, which he put in his pocket wrapped in tissues, he had noted that he was right handed, he forced the fingers around the butt and managed to place the index finger in the trigger guard. He stood back and viewed it, the only snag was the shooting of the hand, he hoped it would be overlooked.

He went to O'Reilly's corpse and placed O'Reilly's weapon in his right hand. At first glance, it appeared that both men had a quarrel which ended fatally for both. John hoped that this would be the assumption initially and possibly be recorded as such. He phoned Diego, told him where he was and asked him if he could get the use of a security armoured vehicle, the type used by banks to ferry cash plus a very secure place where it could be guarded.

Diego replied, "I know the local boss of a security company who has trucks like that, I'll call him but he will insist on his employees being used, drivers and guards."

"Can he and his men keep quiet, can they be trusted?"

"John, I cannot be 100 per cent sure but I will stress how important the matter is, it will take some time, an hour at least."

"Okay, no problem I'll be here." John went to the cellar and began to scan the registers, in one he found a list of names, Spanish and British, opposite were details of sums of money paid with dates and bank account numbers. Some names were familiar. He took possession of all the registers and took all the DVDs, went back to the lounge and waited. He read the same register again until he could memorise many details.

It was nearly two hours before Diego arrived; he was accompanied by a man in plain clothes and two men in uniform. Diego said, "This is Senor Pedro Pizzaro, the branch manager of Safe Security Company."

In Spanish, John said, "Thank you very much, Senor, you are doing a great service, follow me." When all of them entered the lounge, they paused and looked horrified at the two corpses. "The British man is a drug gang boss, the other is a corrupt police officer who was being paid for protecting the drugs boss. Apparently, there must have been an argument resulting in them killing each other." John shrugged, "Such is the fate of evil men. Follow me."

In the cellar, he said, "I want everything to be taken out and placed in the most secure place, there are many items of great value which must be carefully handled, these for example." He showed them the exquisite fragile Faberge eggs worth tens of millions in any currency. "They were all stolen or illegally acquired by other methods. Until they are collected by authorised agents, every item has to be guarded 24 hours a day, can you ensure that this will be done? You will be paid handsomely for the service you provide."

Pizzaro replied, "I assure you, Senor, what you ask for will be done, it is an honour, I have never seen such beautiful works of art."

"Thank you, one more important request, you and your men must not utter one word to anyone which includes family, secrecy is vital. If word gets out; many criminals will attempt to seize these treasures."

"I trust my men, no word of this will be spoken about."

John and Diego assisted in the removal of the safe's contents. When the removal was completed, John informed Pizzaro that he and his men would receive several thousand euros each after all items had been handed over. John and Diego remained when the security staff had left. He showed Diego the register and asked him to have every page photocopied discreetly, better photocopy the other registers too. He divided the DVDs and said, "Look at them, they show the sexual activities that took place here, there will be a number of important personnel performing, you may recognise them. I am only interested in officials, politicians, law enforcement officers, police, lawyers, judges as such, those showing pop stars, actors and actresses etc., destroy. Those you are not sure of, place in a separate pile from those you recognise, also split the nationalities, Spanish, British and others in different piles. I will be doing the same, I want this done as soon as possible."

"I will do it as soon as I get back to the apartment."

"I will be doing the same, it's going to be a busy, long night, I want it all done by the morning and the photocopying done as soon as the shops open."

"Okay, John, what happened here tonight?" He nodded towards the corpses.

"Lovers quarrel," was the reply. Both roared with laughter.

"John, I have never known anyone like you, these last few days, I have learnt so much, it has been a lifetime education."

"Diego, without your assistance, I doubt whether I would have succeeded so soon. Before, I did not have friends, only acquaintances but you truly have become a great friend, I will cherish our friendship for the rest of my life. Now is there any late-night bar open where we can get food and drink?"

"Yes, I know one that is open all night, they play cards in a back room; they have food."

Diego rode pillion holding two large plastic bags containing the DVDs and registers. In a backstreet in the town they entered a small bar, three tables and chairs outside on the pavement, four tables inside. Pints of draught San Miguel and several medium-sized dishes of tapas, tortilla, meatballs, Serrano ham and a large helping of French fries, a small dish of very bitter olives and a dish of cashew nuts were placed on the table. John was famished, the adrenaline had not dissipated. Two more pints of beer and then they left, John dropped Diego at his lodgings, a studio apartment then with his bag of DVDs went on to the hotel, parked and entered reception carrying the large plastic bag.

Maria gazed at him toting the bag, he went to the desk, "Maria, I will be busy most of the night in my room, can I have a pot of coffee sent to the room every hour?"

"Yes, I will see to it, what will you be doing?" He grinned,

"Watching porn." He laughed at her look of disbelief. "I will be watching the sexual antics of many people, some very notable persons, perhaps I will pick up some ideas." He smiled at her. "Darling, the assignment is nearly over, have you watched the TV today?"

She nodded and commented, "All day, on every channel it is about drug raids in England." It then dawned on her and her eyes opened wide, she spoke quietly, "You were involved, you're the one investigating here?"

"Yes, Diego and I are the ones who are responsible, it is only a matter of tying up a few loose ends, I will tell you the full story when I have finally finished."

She said, "It must have been dangerous for you both?"

"I kept Diego out of harm's way, as for myself, I am far too experienced to take risks, besides I have too much to live for."

She replied, "Really?"

"Maria, would I tell you lies, my foes were the ones in danger, not me."

"John, I am glad you did not tell anything, I would have been so worried." She looked at him cheekily, "Being up all night will make you tired, so I work hard in the morning to wake you up."

"I will go to the apartment as soon as I have finished, I am sure I will be up to it." He murmured in her ear, "Will you be ready?"

She whispered, "I am ready now."

"I better go and get to work, don't forget the coffee, I love you."

As soon as he entered, he switched the TV and DVD player on, inserted a DVD and commenced to view it. He only watched a little of each one taking notes on the hotel notepad provided. He identified a few prominent figures, identified show business celebrities, four separate piles, Spanish, British and other nationalities, unknown but suspected of being a noted person and the celebrities pile, if any celebrity was engaged sexually with any notable, the DVD was placed in either the first or second pile. The time passed so quickly that he was surprised when there was a knock at the door. He opened it, Maria pushed a tea trolley in; on it was the coffee, crockery for two, two plates of sandwiches, salmon and cucumber, cheese and onion, tuna, egg plus a plate of cakes and biscuits.

"It is my rest break, I have it with you." She put her arms around his neck and kissed him on the mouth. She whispered, "We have time." She kept kissing him, opening her mouth, her tongue darting in his. The inevitable occurred, he had a big reaction. "Bloody hell, Maria, I am rampant, I feel grotty, I need a shower then I will fuck you so hard that you will beg me to stop."

"That will not happen, come we shower." They undressed in record time, clothes flung here and there. They hurried to the shower, she pulled him, holding a particular very firm part of his anatomy. In the shower, as soon as it was turned on, she placed her hands against the wall, back towards him and stooped slightly with her shapely bottom sticking out. She clutched his cock and placed it in her vagina. "Darling, fuck me hard." He gripped her hips and plunged in and out of her, holding her tight against him, his blood raging. "Oh, yes, my love, it is so good, oh, oh I come, my darling," she kept pushing back against him. She kept talking, "I come again, oh, oh, yes, yes, fuck me, hard my love," her voice rising in tone, he felt the tenseness. "I am coming now," he yelled and held her tight as he came in several spurts.

Both were gasping, when he came out of her warm, sticky opening, they straightened up and held each other tight. She tongued his ear and muttered, "I like that way, your cock feels so big and it goes so deep, did you like it too?"

"Maria, my darling, I love it but I love just being inside you, you really are the sexiest woman, it is fantastic making love to you."

The coffee was still quite hot, they sat naked eating and drinking, she said, "I dress now." He watched her, bikini lace trimmed panties first, matching bra, blouse, neck tie, knee-length pencil skirt which showed her shapely form, she combed her hair, touched up her face and eyes and last of all her shoes. She had watched him eying her, "You like watching me dress?"

"Maria, I like watching you whatever you are doing but yes, watching you dress is very sexy for me."

She came over, held his naked body tight, "Good, I like you watching me." She tugged him and left laughing.

He put his boxers on and got back to his viewing. Two more pots of coffee and he was finished. The time was after 5 a.m. He phoned Huntsman and related all that had occurred, when he told him about the contents of the safe, Huntsman was excited, "My god, you have solved several mysteries from all over Europe, the insurance companies will be ecstatic. I will send the best security team there is to collect the valuables. Financial experts will work on the offshore accounts, I am certain we will get back every penny. As for those persons exhibiting their sexual prowess, they have exposed themselves, they are all threats to their positions, there will be many resignations and firing. They made themselves very vulnerable to blackmail.

"Boss, I have requests, the security firm that is guarding the valuables should be paid well for their assistance. Diego has been fantastic, if it wasn't for him the job would have taken so much longer and perhaps not turned out so well, he should be rewarded."

"I concur, all will be paid excellent sums. Talking about rewards, your payments from insurance companies will be massive, 10 million pounds at least."

John thought for a minute and said, "Did Otter and Badger have families?"

"Yes, both were married, Otter had three children aged 2, 5 and 9 years. Badger had two children aged 8 and 13 years. Both families have been taken care of, they will never want for anything, the children will receive the finest education."

"I am glad to hear that, whatever my reward is I want each family to have a million pounds. Will you please arrange it?"

"Yes, of course." Huntsman thought, *my god, they don't make them like Chameleon any more, what a remarkable man.* He said, "Are you finished over there?"

"Just tying up loose ends; today I will go and see the Guardia Civil commander of the region and give him copies of a register which you will receive in due course. There are many names of different nationalities but predominantly

Spanish and English who are on O'Reilly's payroll detailing the amounts they received, quite a few well-known names."

"Good grief, the establishment will be rocked. I have been summoned to two meetings this morning, an early meeting with the PM and the meeting directly afterwards with all the top security men, police officers, customs and excise, border force, the Home Secretary, Tom, Dick, and Harry. I will inform you of the result. Tomorrow I will be coming to Spain, I will see you. As I said, to have a discussion, your delightful fiancé should be there, I am sure she will be interested. Would the two of you come to dinner with me?"

"Yes, of course."

"Wonderful. I shall see you both tomorrow, bye." John thought, *What was the cunning bugger up to, no matter what he has to tell me, I am finished with the job, I want a peaceful life with Maria.*

He phoned reception, spoke to Maria, "Maria, can you get me four litter bags and bring them to me?" A few minutes later, the bags were delivered, "I'm going to the apartment, can you call a taxi for me? I want to take these with me."

She said, "You look very tired, sleep, I promise I not wake you."

"Give me a call at 9, Diego and I have to go to Malaga to see the Guardia boss. After that meeting, I am free for the rest of the day so whatever you want to do, we do, we can see your parents, you decide."

"Okay, darling, I fix, Mama and Papa would like to see us. I am sure, I call Papa later."

"We can take them out for a meal, someplace really nice."

"They would like that."

"Either you or your papa pick the restaurant." The taxi arrived and he left, he went to bed and within minutes was fast asleep.

The Seventh Day

Maria shook him, "Time to get up, go for a shower, I am fixing breakfast." He got out of bed, feeling groggy and padded slowly to the shower. Maria viewed his naked body, "Mmm, not bad for an old guy," and she laughed.

He muttered, "You cheeky girl, you will suffer later." She was still laughing when he entered the shower, he had a cold one which woke him up properly and refreshed him, he shaved, made himself presentable, hair combed, teeth cleaned. He put clean boxers on and went and sat at the breakfast bar. Orange juice, a large cheese omelette, coffee and toast was served up. Maria sat beside him.

"John, you promised to tell me what happened?"

"I did, I will tell you, I hope I don't shock you and you must never ever tell anyone else, not even your parents." He told her everything, the reason why he had come to Marbella, about O'Reilly, Brown, the corrupt police officer, about the events on the yacht and at O'Reilly's villa. She sat in silence as he spoke. He said, "Now you know what kind of man I am, a very ruthless one who disposes of evil people, please don't judge me too harshly."

She stared at him, eyes watery, "Oh, my darling John, all I see is a very good, honest man, an incredible man who has done so much to make the world a better place. O'Reilly's wife was the girl who you loved years ago. Yes?"

"Yes, that was the reason I undertook the assignment, to save her and I failed."

"My dearest, John, you did not fail, she was near death when you came here, you are not the cause of her death, O'Reilly was, he poisoned her with drugs and killed her, you must not feel guilty."

He looked at her, "You really believe that?"

"Yes and you must too, we are going to have a wonderful life together, in a strange way, perhaps it was fate or written in the stars, Susan brought us together and now wherever she is I think she is smiling that she brought us together."

"Maria, you are a wonderful, wise lady, I adore you, I love you, I worship you."

"I know, John, now get ready for your trip to Malaga." She kissed him tenderly, "The sooner you get there, the sooner you are finished. Call me and I will come to Malaga, pick you up and then we go to Mama's."

He rang Diego, "How are you getting on?"

"I am at a photographic shop, just about finished doing the photocopying."

"Great, can you arrange them in different files, accounts, vehicles, locations of the processing places, bring them with you and the piles of DVDs. We'll take them to Malaga for the General. I am at Maria's, pick me up there." He told Diego the address and said, "Can you phone Malaga and arrange a meeting with the general as soon as we can get there, you can say anything you wish as long as we can see him."

"Sure, he will see us, we can be there at 11.30." After the call ended, he mused about Diego's assured reply. "I have not got the whole picture, I have a feeling I have not been informed of everything, Huntsman, the general and Diego are all pieces of the puzzle but I will solve it today."

10 Downing Street

Huntsman was having a private meeting with the Prime Minister and the Home Secretary prior to a meeting being held in the cabinet room. Huntsman was giving a summary of events, the two listeners were astonished and elated with the results. Then Huntsman told them about Chameleon's decision to resign, dismay was all over their faces, a further discussion took place, the PM said, "Do you think he will accept?"

Huntsman replied, "I am sure it will appeal to him but I am not absolutely certain. It all depends on what his fiancé thinks about it. I am going to Spain tomorrow and am meeting both of them, I will call you tomorrow night."

"Do your darndest, without him, it's a non-goer, there is no one else who can fill the position, we better go and deliver the details to the rest who are probably restless wondering what's it all about."

The three of them entered the cabinet room, everyone stood up. "Sit down, refreshments later, this could be a long session so let's start." Those attending were the heads of the security services, special branch, customs and excise, anti-terrorist group, the Commissioner of the Metropolitan Police, the Chief of the City of London police, two HMIs (Her

Majesty's Inspectors of Constabulary, the Border Control group.

The PM opened the meeting, "All of you must be aware of the sensational events that have occurred, the media has been reporting on it, commenting on it and the usual so-called experts have been analysing and giving their usual comments on many of the T.V. panels.

To be brief, the destruction of a vast drug network occurred, hundreds of arrests all over the country and still more to come. The drug mogul, the head of the network, was resident in Spain."

One attendee raised his arm and said, "Was, has he evaded capture and how was this all accomplished. There have been many attempts to bring this man to justice over several years, I am sure all of us would like to know the facts."

The PM replied, "The man sitting to my right will give a full report, a few of you may be aware of him, many of you will not know him, he is known only by a code name, Huntsman, will you please give us your report?"

Huntsman stood up, "I am the head of a covert organisation, a very small group in fact, financed by the government. We undertake difficult operations when others have failed. I heard the comment about years being spent on bringing the drug gang leader without success. Well, the amazing result being shown all over the world was achieved in less than seven days." There was astonishment on the faces of the attendees, one of them, a dapper figure in plain clothes, white collar shirt but with blue stripes, grey three-piece suit, early 60s, black thinning hair that looked dyed, reddish complexion had a derisory look as if he did not believe it.

Huntsman continued, "The head of the drug organisation was Damien O'Reilly, most of you are familiar with the name. An evil, brutal beast suspected of many robberies and murders, his right hand man was Joseph Brown, equally as evil and brutal. I was given the assignment several months ago, I sent two men to Spain to initiate enquiries, two good men, within days they disappeared, presumably killed, this was confirmed in the last few days, Brown and others captured them, he tortured them but cutting of strips of skin before attaching weights to them and dumping them in the sea.

One of my men had left the organisation a year ago, this man code name Chameleon was with me for 14 years. He had a 100 per cent success rate but he walked out, he became a recluse, I kept tabs on him and paid him a visit, I had an ace up my sleeve, so to speak; he had been in a relationship for two years with a lovely girl, because of the job, he broke it off. O'Reilly was suspected of murdering his first two wives, his third wife was destined for the same fate; she had become a junkie, a shadow of her former self, she had been Chameleon's lover six years before, the one he had a two-year relationship with, so he undertook the assignment. He was assisted by a Guardia Civil officer who was working undercover alone, he could not trust any fellow officers."

Huntsman paused, the man with the derisory look, arms folded said, "How long is this going to take, get to the point."

Huntsman said, "Is there anyone else bored as this gentleman obviously is, if there is, you can leave." No response, he said to the man, "Please tell me who you are and what is your profession, if you don't mind?"

The man perked up, "I am Sir Colin Spencer, the head of the UK Customs and Excise. The finest most efficient service in the country."

"Indeed, your pride is commendable, I wish to have a short discussion later, now, if you don't mind, I will continue, now where was I before the interruption, ah yes, my man undertook the assignment. Within days, he had established locations where the drugs were concealed on vehicles destined for the UK. He waited and when drugs were landed from power boats into pickups which were driven to warehouse where the drugs were transferred into large vehicles he transmitted the information to me, together with a great many people the vehicles were tracked when they were in the UK every one of 12 vehicles were followed to their destination and the traps sprung resulting in hundreds of arrests.

Meanwhile, my man had solved the murder of my two men, had hidden himself on O'Relly's yacht when Brown and four others boarded and put to sea, their purpose to dispose of O'Reilly's wife, she had been strangled by O'Reilly. My man dealt with the five of them. Brown, who actually detested O'Reilly, gave valuable information to my man just before the yacht sunk ablaze. All five evil men perished; my man managed to escape."

"Huh, your man killed them, just a common murderer, this is just poppycock."

Huntsman spoke calmly but with a cold tone. "You really have no inkling of the dangers of some assignments, I was going to have a private discussion with you later but now is a favourable time." He noticed a big smile on the special branch man's face, who winked and gave him a thumbs up.

Huntsman began, "You take great pride in your position, do you know your chief officers?"

"Of course, I know them all, excellent men."

"How long have you been the head of the service?"

"Five years."

"Really, that is interesting, then you are familiar with those manning the channel ports and the tunnel?"

"Yes, superb officers, all dedicated, one officer has been offered promotion but he is very happy, very popular, and has been in the same post four years."

"Would that be Desmond O'Donnell, the chief officer of Calais, I did hear he was very good at his job."

"Yes, wonderful man, Dod, we call him, he works so many extra duties, the salt of the earth."

"You have not heard about O'Donnell then?"

Alarmed, he said, "What's happened, has he had an accident?" "

I suppose in the widest sense, one could call it that; actually, he was arrested earlier today by the special branch."

"No, it can't be, it's a mistake."

"O'Donnell's real name is Sean O'Casey; he and O'Reilly were the closest of friends. In their teens, they were very active members of the IRA suspected of a number of killings by sniper fire and bombing. They were arrested several times but released because of the lack of evidence and witnesses who either withdrew their statements or vanished. He is a member of O'Reilly's drug organisation, the vehicles with drugs concealed on them always passed through when O'Casey was on duty, in four years, I just wonder what amounts of drugs passed through, how many people died from overdose, how many crimes committed by drug users desperate for cash to buy drugs, how many overworked hospital staff had to deal with the drug abusers, what would be the estimated cost, several billion pounds is a conservative estimate. You pompous, arrogant moron, I cannot decide whether you are incompetent, negligent or mentally deficient; a combination of all three, I reckon. Special Branch officers are waiting to question you, if I were you, I would put a gun in my mouth and blow my brains out but you are a gutless pathetic weakling, by the way, it was my killer who discovered the facts about O'Casey. My killer is a patriot, a man of integrity. Get out of my sight, hand in your resignation, your knighthood will be taken away."

A voice rang out, the Home Secretary shouted, "Wait, you have not the option of resigning, you are fired herewith and there will be no pension rights. Get out." Spencer slunk out, face now an unhealthy grey pallor. When the door closed behind him, the entire assembly rose to their feet and applauded Huntsman. He bowed his head, "Thank you, I apologise for my outburst but that object really got to me, shall I continue?"

The answer was a unanimous loud, "Yes."

"When I informed my man of the result in England, he went to O'Reilly's villa where the head police officer of Marbella was having a discussion with O'Reilly. Outside, six moonlighting police officers were guarding O'Reilly, they were persuaded to leave; three of them had to have hospital treatment. The result was that O'Reilly and the officer had a quarrel over money and they killed each other, that was the scenario. There was a huge walk-in safe in a cellar, accessed by a hidden entrance behind a cupboard.

The contents of the safe were a large treasure trove of stolen jewellery, which included two Faberge eggs, two famous necklaces, gems of every description, most will be traced to the true owners, I have been in contact with insurance companies. What was more important was the number of registers found, O'Reilly. Kept meticulous records, names of people on his payroll and the amounts he paid, records of all the vehicles and power boats used in the transport of drugs, details of the locations of the drug processing laboratories in Morocco and Algiers. A list of names and telephone numbers in countries around the world, well-known names such as drug cartels. The information will be shared with Drug Enforcement Agencies, there is much more but you have the idea of the importance of the result of this assignment. Are there any questions?"

Hands were raised, the questions were the same, they wanted to know all about Chameleon. "He is simply the most brilliant agent I have ever come into contact with. He was an orphan had a very disturbed childhood, joined the boys military service, was in the army for 12 years, fought in many actions, has a remarkable record, been decorated many times, attained the rank of Major, an officer I knew told me that he was leaving the army. I had just taken over the organisation, the calibre of some of my men was questionable and I was desperate for good men. I interviewed him, he agreed to join and the rest is history. His code name Chameleon says much. He can blend into any background, mix with people at any level; he is a brilliant linguist, speaks many languages and dialects, it is a natural gift, has the top class of black belts in all the martial arts, is a cracksman with many firearms. He does not use many disguises, he adopts different body movements, postures, walking, talking. He keeps himself to himself, no close friends, had the two-year relationship, has had a few brief encounters with women. He became a recluse when he left up to the time I came back into his life.

He thinks I am a heartless bastard, that is the fate of one who gives orders. I think the world of him, I am in awe of his achievements, I admire him so much. Yes, he has killed, he can be a stone cold killer but he has made the world a better place by eliminating monsters. He is decisive, he can plan and execute his work so well, he makes things look so easy. In my opinion he is the best agent in the world, on a different level from anyone else. I can talk about him for hours but I will stop, just one more bit of news, this is his last assignment, he is engaged to be married in the near future, he wants to settle down, breed horses and raise a family. It will be impossible to replace him but I fully support his decision, what he has achieved for this country will never be equalled. Not one of us in this room is his equal and I am not demeaning any of you. Thank you for allowing me to talk for so long."

There was a clamour of voices all asking the same question, "Can't he be persuaded to remain in your organisation? The country cannot afford to lose such a man."

Huntsman replied, "The Prime Minister, Home Secretary and I had a meeting just prior to this one and they came up with a brilliant idea." He nodded to the PM. "Sir, would you care to explain your plan?"

"Thank you, Alex, I will. I agree with all of you we cannot allow Chameleon to go, listen to my proposal at the conclusion. I want a show of hands to show approval. I want to establish a school, college, whatever. To buy a large residence in a remote part, such as Scotland, modernise it and add many facilities, to have the finest team of tutors, specialists in weapons, martial arts, surveillance, interrogation, techniques in disguise, experts in rock climbing, scuba diving and so on. To recruit from every level of society, many candidates will probably come from the armed forces and the police. I know that many organisations run courses, the police have Bramshillfor senior command courses, MI 5 and MI6 have historically recruited graduates from Oxford and Cambridge universities, the special branch is a police department and so on, there has never been such an institute as I am proposing. Alex with be the head but the Director of Training, we hope will be Chameleon who will choose the location and will be on the selection and examining panel for recruits. He will impart his knowledge in lectures, he will choose the teachers, instructors and he will also visit agents on assignments; he will be 2.i.c. to Alex. He will have family quarters at the school. That is a very brief summary but it should give you an idea of what I want, a super establishment for agents. Please raise your arms if you support the project."

Everyone raised their arms, "Good, any questions?"

"Will Chameleon take the position?"

"Alex and I think he will, the course will be of three months duration, only two courses per annum. This gives him the opportunity to pursue his interests, such as breeding horses and his wife will be with him. The courses will not have large numbers of candidates and we estimate the failure rate will be high, all of them will sign the Official Secrets Act before they set foot on the place, those who fail will not dare to utter a word about the establishment. Alex is going to Spain tomorrow to meet with Chameleon who will be given time to think it over. If he accepts, he will start looking for a suitable building soon. I ask all of you one thing, within your departments, if you have a likely candidate, contact Alex, he will arrange and check the antecedence from birth, every aspect of the background will be analysed, political extremists, far right or far left will not be considered."

"What about women candidates?"

"There is no bar for them, there will be accommodation facilities for them, I do hope we recruit women. It's time for refreshments." He pressed a buzzer, immediately the door opened, staff wheeled in trolleys loaded with tea and coffee pots, crockery, plates of sandwiches, Danish pastries, doughnuts, plain and fancy ones. "Help yourself." From the PM, he went around chatting, answering questions, Huntsman was asked many questions about Chameleon but one question was, "The PM called you Alex, I assume that's your real name?"

"Quite correct," he did not venture any further details. The meeting ended shortly afterwards.

Malaga

Just after the Downing Street meetings commenced, Diego picked John up who had two lots of DVDs, the Spanish and the unknowns. On the back seat, he saw separate files of documents, each file stapled; two bags of DVDs were on the floor. As he slid onto the front seat, he said, "All set."

Diego replied, "The general will see us as soon as we arrive."

"Does he know the reason for our visit?"

"Yes, I told him it was all about the drug bust and about O'Reilly, he is very eager to see you."

"He's not going to clamp me in irons, is he?"

Diego roared, "I don't think so."

Their arrival at the Guardia Civil headquarters had been forewarned. Diego stopped at the steps in front of the entrance. They picked up the bags of DVDs and the files, only to be dispossessed of them; an officer drove the car off to a parking spot. An officer with badges of rank told them to accompany him. He took them to the third floor, rapped on a door. A loud entrar and he ushered them in. A tall well-built figure in a well-tailored uniform, two rows of medal ribbons adorned the left of his shirt, stood in front of a large wooden desk. Face hewn out of stone, he shook hands with them, he indicated two chairs. "Sit down please," he said in English.

He looked at John and said with a smile, "So, you are the catalyst who lit the fire?"

John had already worked out certain details, he replied with a grin, "General, you know that, you know my boss, known as Huntsman and you detailed Diego to assist me."

Diego flushed and said, "John, I wanted to tell you."

"That's okay, amigo, you are an excellent officer and man, your loyalty does you credit and your assistance was invaluable, we made a great team, I just hope you are appreciated and justly rewarded." He then spoke to the general, "Your English is excellent, I assume you attended courses in England and that is probably where you met Huntsman."

"Correct, may I say, you are everything that Alex said you were, he gave you such a fantastic reference that I found it hard to believe. I now believe every word, your achievements here are incredible. I wish to thank you. Diego is one of my best men and I did detail him to assist you and also to safeguard you, which was totally unnecessary. You kept him safe and carried out the dangerous actions alone. For your information, it has been recorded that O'Reilly and Cordoba shot and killed each other, case closed. The DVDs and the copies of the registers are being examined now. Operations will take place soon to destroy the processing plants. The powerboats and all the vehicles used will be seized and those who used them arrested. Those filmed on the DVDs will be advised, no doubt there will be resignations and sackings. Any officers identified will be crucified. The Marbella police will be taken apart and any who were employed by O'Reilly will be disciplined, fined, reprimanded and posted to another area."

"You have got everything covered, General, thank you for assigning Diego, he has become a great friend."

The General put on a civilian jacket, "This calls for a celebration, come, there is a nice bar and restaurant in the next street." The Pescador specialised in seafood but served other foods. They sat on the covered terrace and had coffees and brandy, a variety of tapas. John was surprised when the general said, "When is the wedding?" John looked at Diego, "Diego did not tell me, Ramon is one of my dearest friends since boyhood. Maria is a wonderful girl, Ramon and Rosita are so happy." He smiled. "I have been invited to the wedding, Maria and you are a perfect couple, I have known her from her birth, Ramon and Rosita were concerned, they had visions of her never getting wed; suddenly, everything changed, all within days."

"General you referred to my boss as Alex, I have only known him as Huntsman, you know who he is, would you tell me his name, by the way, I will be inviting him to the wedding."

"That is wonderful, he will be so happy. I will tell you what I know but never let him know I told you; he is a very private person. I have known him for at least 20 years, we are good friends, he comes to Spain every year and I have a vacation in Scotland, he has a large estate in Scotland, in a beautiful area with a river running through the grounds, we fish for salmon and trout, drink a great deal of malt whisky and talk.

"He was married, a lovely lady, they adored each other. They were childless though they tried, they accepted the fact that they would never have children, they lived for each other. Tragically, seven years ago, Isabel died of cancer. Alex was heartbroken, it took a long time for him to get back to normal. Every Christmas, her birthday, their wedding anniversary… he places red roses on her grave. She is buried on the estate."

John had a big lump in his throat, he said, "I never realised, I always thought he was an unemotional, heartless man, how wrong can a person be? I feel bloody awful and I feel so sad about his wife."

"Alex has talked about you so much, he regrets assigning you to so many missions but he had no choice, he knew that you would succeed, you never failed. Please never let him know but he has always regarded you as the son he never had, he is so proud of you, he has a great affection for you but he will never display it in your presence. He is a proud man, a very good man, he cares so much for you and the rest of his men.

His full name is Alexander Gordon Hamilton, Earl of Selkirk, he comes from an ancient lineage, going back to the sixth or seventh century. He knows everything about your background, your mother abandoning you, your tough childhood, the fostering of you. He knows of your attempts to trace your mother. He carried out so many enquiries to trace her, hiring the best investigators but the result was the same. All the records were destroyed in a fire."

John was lost for words, he felt so humble and terrible that he was so wrong. He said, "I am so glad you told me, I won't say a word about this. This has been an extraordinary week, the highlight of my life, I have learnt so much and I am going to marry the most wonderful lady. I am so glad to have met you, thank you."

"It has been a special occasion for me, I hope to see Alex when he comes here. He should arrive tomorrow morning at about 10. I have arranged for him to be picked up and taken to the El Dorado hotel in Marbella. He will call you the moment he is in Marbella."

"For the first time I am looking forward to seeing him."

"He has much to discuss with you, after you have ended your talk, please ask him to contact me?"

"I will do, excuse me, Maria, will pick me up from here, I must call her." He made the call and 10 minutes later, she arrived and stopped next to the bar terrace. When she saw the general, she looked surprised, "Tio Juan, I did not know you were the one John was meeting."

"Maria, my dear, you look radiant, more beautiful than I have ever seen you, it must be because of your man here. We have had a wonderful meeting, keep a tight hold of him, he is a special person."

"I intend to, Papa has spoken to you, yes?"

"He has indeed, Teresa, the boys and I are coming to the wedding, we are delighted, Teresa was wondering if she would ever see such a day."

"Tio, we are going to see Mama and Papa now, I look forward to seeing you all soon."

"Do you have a date yet?"

"It will be arranged today." John shook the general's hand then spoke to Diego, "I'll call you, when Maria is at work we'll have a drink, okay?"

"Sure." Maria and he then left.

In the car, she told him that she spoken with the hotel manager and he had agreed to her having time off when she required it in regard to the wedding preparations, she then said, "John, what do you think? I would like to carry on working until I get pregnant, I could have time off when we are looking for a ranch."

"Darling it is up to you, I am not sure yet about doing any more assignments, there is a lot to think about."

He smiled, "I hope you get pregnant and soon, we'll just have to practise a lot, you do want to practise don't you?"

She chuckled. "Every moment we can."

Ramon and Rosita were delighted to see them, wine and food were already on the table. They talked about the wedding preparations and the date; agreement was reached that the ceremony would be in two weeks on a Saturday. Invitations would be sent out in two days' time, Ramon had already spoken to the priest, and the manager of The Mirador Hotel which was cited on a hill overlooking Malaga, a preliminary reservation had been made. John offered to give a cash advancement but Ramon refused, "Pay me later after the wedding." Maria mentioned that John had been at a meeting with her Uncle Juan. Ramon peered at John and was keen to know the reason but he just said, "Juan is my friend, he is a good man, a very good officer." Maria and Mama discussed Maria's dress and the bridesmaids dresses; they would go on a shopping spree soon. John mused, *The preparations were all in hand, all he had to do was turn up suitably dressed.*

They left about 4 o'clock; on the way back, Maria said, "John, it's only two weeks to the wedding, I can stop taking the birth control pills now, if we have a baby a little early we just say it is premature."

"No, Maria, I am not going to tempt fate, who knows I could be struck by lightning, be struck down crossing a road, no, definitely not, if I was killed or died before we were married and you were pregnant, what would people say, we can wait two more weeks, on our wedding night, then you stop taking pills."

Maria thought, *John is thinking about his mother and how he was abandoned.* She said, "It was only an idea and you are right, I love you, John, we will wait until we are married." She added mischievously, "We have time for a quickie, yes?"

He laughed, "You are a sexy witch, I am under your spell forever."

At the apartment, they were intimate with a variation, he sat on the settee and she sat on his lap with her back to him as she lowered her body onto him and rode him. Both climaxed quickly, they showered and then he watched her get dressed. "Maria, I can watch you forever, you are the most desirable beautiful woman in the world."

She laughed, "I promise you on our wedding night, I will be dressed in very sexy underwear, you will like."

"My love, you would be desirable wearing a paper bag." He walked with her to the hotel, called Diego and met him an hour later. Both were relaxed now that the assignment was over; they just had a pleasant chat, had a good meal, a couple of more beers then called it a night.

The Eighth Day

In the morning, John was asleep when Maria slid into bed and did her usual coaxing him awake, not that he needed much coaxing. They stayed in bed for about two hours, showered, had breakfast and went out for a stroll. Just two people besotted with each other, hand in hand, arm in arm. They had churros and hot chocolate for dipping the churros.

At 11.20, John received a call from Huntsman. "Hi, boss, I assume you are in Marbella?"

"Yes, can we meet soon, I have a great deal to talk about to you. Please bring Maria, she will be interested in what I have to say."

"Okay, where and when?"

"Come to The El Dorado, it's on the beach road, make it for 12.30, I will order lunch for us; after we eat we, can talk in my room."

"Okay, see you soon."

John told Maria who said, "What is he like?"

"Maria, I had opinions about him which were unfavourable; I was so wrong about him, let's hear what he has to say."

They entered the hotel exactly on time. Huntsman was waiting, a dapper figure, wearing a beige linen two-piece suit, white shirt, red bow tie, a Panama straw hat in one hand, highly-polished lace-up brown shoes. He came to them, smiling broadly, "It's good to see you and, you, my dear Maria are simply the most beautiful lady I have ever had the honour of meeting. I understand perfectly why this extraordinary man has fallen head over heels in love with you. Come, lunch has been ordered." He led the way into a dining room to a reserved table. Two bottles of wine, red and white, were already uncorked. The waiter took their orders. Wine poured, Huntsman raised his glass, "To you both, to your wedding, may you have a long and healthy life and many lovely children, I wish you the best of everything, you certainly deserve it."

John said, "Thank you, boss, as you know I was a bit of a loner, I had no real friends in the UK. Maria and I would really like you to attend our wedding in just over two weeks' time, please say yes, you and a Spanish friend and his family will be my only guests."

Huntsman was very moved and it showed, "Thank you so much for the invitation, I am honoured and very happy, yes I want to attend very, very much."

John had a sudden thought, "Would you stand with me at the altar as my best man?"

"You have honoured me more and more; I will be proud and happy to do so. This has turned out to be quite a day and we have only started."

They started eating their meals, Maria asked Huntsman, "What can I call you, Huntsman sounds a bit strange?"

He laughed. "You are quite right my dear, my name is Alexander, shortened to Alex, please call me Alex."

"Alex, John has never really spoken about you, do you have a family?"

"Maria, I was married to a wonderful, lovely lady, we never had children because of a medical condition so Isabel and I just lived for each other, we doted and loved each other so much. Tragically, she died seven years ago after suffering from cancer for two years. I still really have not been able to come to terms with her passing. I miss her every single minute of the day."

Maria stretched and took his hand, she had tears in her eyes, "Oh, Alex, I am so very sorry."

Alex's eyes were watery, he said, "Thank you for your kind words, you are a very caring, wonderful person."

John was choked up. "Boss, I didn't know, I too am so sorry."

"I had my work and I used that to keep me occupied, I think it saved my sanity; my interest in your successful exploits kept me going. I understand why you are leaving, I would in your position, Maria and you have a wonderful life ahead of you."

"Boss, why did you come here, I have a feeling that you are up to something?"

"You always did have that sixth sense, you are correct, there are two separate issues, the first is a proposition, the second is more personal. Let us go to my room where it is more comfortable, we can raid the fridge and have something stronger to drink."

Revelations

Once they had settled, Alex sat in an armchair opposite Maria and John who were sitting on a settee close together. Alex started by telling them about the meetings with the PM and Home Secretary about the plan to establish a school to recruit the finest agents, the finest team of tutors ever assembled. About the desired location, residential quarters and facilities. "The people at the meeting, the top professional people in England were in favour but there was one important condition, the only person they want to run it is you. Before you decline, please consider the proposal and don't give me your decision now. I would be in overall charge but really only a figurehead to rubber stamp your decisions.

You would have a blank cheque, unlimited funds, you would have to travel around to choose a suitable place, it would have to be a large residence, modernised to the highest standards, single rooms for the candidates, en suite shower, TV, DVD, desktop computer, lavish living quarters for Maria and you. Set in extensive grounds remote from the nearest residential area by a few miles. There are stately homes and castles on the market, renovation and installing the facilities would be done. An indoor swimming pool, a large one, a climbing wall, firing ranges outdoor and indoor to be built, a gymnasium, a fitness room, medical facilities etc are all essential. You would supervise the installation of every facility.

Only two courses per annum, each of three months duration, this would allow you to live in Spain between courses, also it would be a four and a half day week, so you could fly to Spain to visit Maria's parents and check on the running of your ranch. You would be my deputy but you would be in charge of the teaching staff, you would be expected to take classes yourself to teach your expertise. An administrator would be appointed to do most of the paperwork. Regular assessments by your staff and yourself, it is estimated that there would be a failure rate, quite a high one; the courses would only have a maximum of 20 students. Those who pass would be assigned to field operations anywhere in the world, You would have to pay them visits to check on them, to advise them. The object of all this is to create a superior covert force, finer than any other in the world. Staff and trainees/students will sign the Official Secrets Act. If you accept, Maria would accompany you visiting potential sites, she would also furnish and outfit your living quarters.

Your salary would be one million pounds per annum, with an increment every year, your accommodation and meals would be free, two cars will be provided, the latest Range Rover for you and a medium-sized saloon for Maria. Initially, you will be very busy, I will give you assistance whenever you require it, we will discuss all potential staff appointments. Talk it over with Maria, take your time, I will be staying several days. Let us have a drink before I continue."

John had been looking at Maria during Alex's talk, her eyes were shining and she had given the slightest nod, she was definitely in favour of his acceptance; truth be told he liked the concept, he would employ a ranch foreman experienced with horse breeding, he would purchase a large ranch with staff quarters. The more he thought about it, the more he liked it. Maria and he would discuss it later.

Alex and John had beer; Maria drank water. Alex continued. "When you joined my group, I got copies of your military record which included a copy of your birth certificate. Very scant details on it, father and mother unknown, I learnt that you had hired private investigators over the years trying to trace your mother, not your father. The story you believed was that as a new-born baby, you were left outside a hospital entrance. I became interested in you. I too hired the very best investigators without success. I believe there is much truth in genetics. You were simply the best agent I had, you have the lot, intelligence, initiative, coolness, determination; now, I find out you have a love of horses and animals. I wondered where you inherited these qualities, from your mother or father.

One of my best friends, we were at Eton and Oxford University, is Sir William Montrose who lives in the South of Scotland, he has a lovely estate, on the borders of mine, I gather you know my name?"

"I did hear something about you belonging to the aristocracy."

"My name is Alexander Gordon Hamilton, Earl of Dunbar, Will is married to a beautiful woman, Fiona, maiden name Falconer. Will and I see each other regularly, being neighbours. We were having a chat a few days ago and I commented that Fiona was one of the great Scottish beauties and extremely elegant and kind and I said 'I always detect a wistfulness, a slight sadness in her, am I right in thinking that'?"

"Yes, you are quite right, please, never let Fiona know I told you." He then commenced telling me a story, a tragic, sad tale.

"Fiona was 15 years, an only child of Lord Robert Falconer, Duke of Arran, he was a stern man and he adored Fiona, unknown to him she was in love with the son of her father's closest friend, the father was Duncan McEwen, the Earl of Berwick, The son, Adam, was 21 years of age, a handsome youth, very talented, very intelligent, he was a student at St Andrews University, all studies came easy to him, he had a gift of learning several foreign languages." When he heard this John felt shivers, he suspected where this was leading.

"Adam was destined for a career in the foreign office. Fiona and he were madly in love and as soon as she was 18 years, they intended to marry. Their relationship was a secret, neither of their families had any inkling. Adam was an excellent horseman, he rode as often as he could with the fox hunting packs, he loved the exciting chase across the countryside, jumping over hedges, ditches and so on. He never viewed the killing of the fox, he loved animals. One day he met with the pack to ride with them. On this day, his regular mount had gone a little lame so he picked a stallion, he had ridden it before, he knew it was skittish but had always controlled it. As the hunt was cantering along a lane bordered by hedgerows, a pheasant suddenly flew up right in front and close to Adam's horse's head. It was so sudden, the horse reared and threw Adam who landed on his head, breaking his neck, killed instantly.

A tragic freak accident, Adam was an only child. Both families were devastated. Fiona discovered she was pregnant, she was frantic; she kept quiet until it began to show, she was terrified and never told anyone. One night she left with a few clothes packed in a bag and went to Glasgow, her mind in a befuddled state, nothing planned, not knowing what to do. In

Glasgow, she was found huddled in a shop doorway by two police constables. They questioned her and asked what her name was, she would not give them any details to the officers, they took her to a convent in the area. The convent, a strict order, took in waifs and strays, in particular, pregnant teenagers. There was a very strict rule, there were no facilities for children. As soon as a child was born, it was taken away there and then, the mother never knew then, she was never told where the baby was sent to. A cruel practice. Whether when Fiona gave birth, it was botched or not, Fiona discovered she could never have another child.

When she discovered her child had been taken away, she went crazy, they feared for her mentality, also she was very ill. She was in the convent hospital for months; it was feared she would never recover good health. The convent had an arrangement with an orphanage, all babies were sent there, ironically it was a strict presbyterian institute, it was a grim Victorian building, a birth certificate in the name of John Knox was issued; the baby was there for a few months and then fostered out, brought back, fostered again until the boy eventually found a decent home with good foster parents. Fiona never knew for some time whether she had a boy or a girl, it was much later that a nun told her she had a boy.

As soon as her parents found she was gone, they were very worried and baffled, they contacted their close friends, the McEwen's. They got together and tried to solve the puzzle. Domestic staff at both residences were questioned, the staff seem to know more than the families, from the servants they learnt about the romance and a middle-aged maid employed by Fiona's father said she thought Fiona had been pregnant, she had heard the bouts of morning sickness.

Fiona's parents were overcome with fear of her safety, very, very upset, the father realised that his stern attitude was a factor, that she had been frightened to tell him, he felt an immense guilt and sadness. He immediately hired the best private investigators who made enquiries everywhere, Glasgow, Edinburgh, all the towns in the Clyde and Forth valleys. It was months later that she was found doing menial tasks in a children's home. She was persuaded to return home where she was embraced so lovingly. Now the same investigators were hired to find the boy. They visited the convent but only the Mother Superior spoke to them, she would not divulge anything or she did not know which girl had given birth. Under threat of a court order, she eventually gave them the orphanage details, unfortunately, there had been a fire that destroyed part of the premises a few months prior. All the records, paperwork had been destroyed. It was a dead end."

He looked at John who had sat, tensed up, a sad look on his face. Alex said, "Now you know you were never abandoned, your mother and your grandparents did everything they could to trace you." The tears streamed down John's face as he spoke with a hoarse voice, "I now know the truth."

Alex said, "When Will told me, I told him I knew Fiona's son but to prove it absolutely I told him to get a sample of Fiona's hair, place it in an envelope but not to tell Fiona yet. He did so and I hurried back to your house. I effected an entry and got a sample of your hair, I took the samples to a laboratory in Edinburgh, exercised pressure. I do have some influence, they did DNA tests, the result was positive, I returned to Will's and I informed Fiona all about you. She seemed to shed years, she and both sets of grandparents are anxious to see you, yes the grandparents are all alive, in their eighties but well."

John, his face tear-stained said, "I can never, ever possibly thank you enough."

Alex smiled, "No thanks are necessary, I am just so happy for you and the families waiting to see you, Maria, do you have a passport?"

"Yes."

"Wonderful, I have already booked three flights to Edinburgh, we fly out at 9 a.m. We have a meeting at 2 p.m. at the Hilton Hotel." He took out his smartphone, "I have some pictures for you, of your mother and father." He showed them to John and Maria, pictures of Fiona through the years and what she looked like now, when they saw the picture of Adam, they were taken aback, the resemblance of father and son was remarkable, no one could deny the family connection after seeing the picture. Alex remarked, "The two of you are like peas out of the same pod."

Maria hugged Alex, "You are a wonderful, caring man. When we have children, you will be their Godfather."

Alex had tears in his eyes, "Maria, I would be proud and honoured, thank you. my dear."

John was shaking his head, "This has to be the most incredible day of my life, no, the most incredible week of my life and it's all because of you, I met Maria and found out the truth about my mother, something that has haunted me all my life."

Alex said, "Tonight, we will have the greatest celebration, Maria, would your parents do us the honour of attending?"

"I am sure but I will call them now." She made the call and asked Alex, "Where and when?"

"Here at 8.30."

"They are coming, thank you, Alex."

"It has been quite an occasion, I am going to have a rest now, I will see tonight." John looked at Maria, she nodded and said, "Tell Alex now."

John said, "Boss, Alex, I would love to take the position, we'll make a great team," and he gave a broad smile.

"Splendid, oh, that is just stupendous, I'll ring the PM today, what a fantastic day." Maria and John left the room.

Alex phoned the PM and told him that John had accepted the position, the PM and stated he would inform the Home Secretary who would then pass the news on for recruiting purposes. Alex received instructions to pay the security firm and Diego, "Give them cheques, you will be reimbursed."

Alex said, "Regarding Chameleon, he is getting married in two weeks' time, with the honeymoon I don't expect him to start for about six weeks."

"No problem, just tell me the date he will start and the contract will be completed, please give him and his bride my best wishes."

Alex requested the receptionist to call for a taxi. He asked the driver to take him to the safe security premises. There he requested to see Senor Pizzaro, when Pizzaro appeared, Alex introduced himself and said, "You and your guards performed a very important service for my man, here is a cheque in appreciation of your service, I hope it is satisfactory."

Pizzaro looked at the sum and smiled, "Fantastico, gracias."

"A security team is on its way to take possession of the items, thank you again." He then left.

Maria and John strolled arm in arm, he said, "It's a dream come true, I feel like I am floating."

She clutched his arm tight, "I'll make sure you won't float away."

He kissed her softly. "I love you so very much."

"I know, I love you my dearest, darling John." She whispered, "Can we relax when we get back."

He grinned, "Define what you mean by relaxing?"

"Oh. just having a lie down for an hour or so."

He laughed. "My love, my idea and your idea of relaxing are not exactly the same but I like your idea better." They did relax but only after a bout of mildly strenuous lovemaking.

The dinner that night was a great success, General Juan Fernandez and his wife Teresa also attended. It was a joyous occasion, Alex charmed Ramon and Rosita. John and Maria told them about the position he had accepted, they were excited. Juan was very interested in the project and remarked that with Alex and John running it, success was guaranteed. After coffees and brandies, Alex made a statement astounding everyone, he said to John, "You do realise that you are the heir to two of the most successful estates in Scotland plus two other smaller estates. Fiona's father breeds cattle and sheep, your father's family breeds horses, rare breeds plus cattle.

Both estates are run by excellent managers and staff. The two smaller estates are equally well run, one is your step-father's estate; the other is mine, I have no relatives. I want to leave it to someone who will appreciate it, Juan will tell you it is a beautiful scenic area. You will be the wealthiest man in Scotland, possibly in the whole of the UK. All of us will engage the most brilliant legal team to ensure that no or a very small sum of death duties are paid. All the residences are in top class condition, all modernised but retaining the comfort and charm of another age. Maria, my dear you will love all of them and no doubt will spend periods in them all."

John's mind was in a daze, he was speechless, he just shook his head in amazement. He realised that he would become busy paying visits but they were all in Southern Scotland and the school would be in Scotland, he would also have a ranch in Andalucia but with good management teams, his personal involvement would be limited to occasional visits. He could handle it. He stood up, "This day has been sensational, thank you for helping. Maria and I celebrate, you are all special people, in two weeks we will all be celebrating again. Tomorrow, I am going to meet the one person in my life that has been an obsession my whole life in trying to trace her, my mother, needless to say, it will be a very emotional event. Alex, I owe it all to you, you are an incredible man. Thank you." Everyone applauded.

Before the party broke up, Alex reminded John and Maria of the early start in the morning, he told them he would arrange a taxi and pick them up at 6. Maria told him the address. He then handed a cheque to John, "Please give this to Diego when you see him, it is in appreciation of the invaluable assistance he gave you, I have already given Senor

Pizzaro a cheque for a similar amount." John saw the sum of 50,000 euros, he said Diego would be very happy and that it would be unexpected, he thanked Alex, bade him goodnight.

Maria and John walked to the apartment in absolute bliss. They went straight to bed, John set the alarm for 5 a.m. They held each other tight, lying in bed, then matters became heated resulting in a passionate session which exhausted them, they fell asleep clasped in each other's arms around 1 a.m.

The Ninth Day

Alex was bang on time. They had one large holdall in which they had packed changes of clothing and toiletries; they each carried hand luggage. The flight was a direct one and landed in Edinburgh after 12 noon. Alex told them he had reserved rooms at the hotel for them for three nights, "I think you will extend your visit longer; everyone will want you to visit them, there will be so many welcome parties but you will be staying at different places so three nights should be sufficient, no doubt Maria would like to do some shopping and visit the sights in Edinburgh."

"Thank you, Alex, I would love to visit the shops and I want to visit the castle too." They booked in at the hotel, Alex told them he would call at 1.50. Their room was spacious, beautifully furnished, a welcome bottle of Champagne in an ice bucket, glasses plus a basket of fruit were on a sideboard. Maria said, "First, we shower then we have Champagne." In the shower, they went into a clinch, open mouthed kissing, tongues down each other's throat. "Darling, I am so hot, I am on fire, I need your cock." Her hands flat against the wall, she wiggled her bottom invitingly. "I want it now deep inside me." He clasped her hips and thrust inside her, she pressed against his groin as he penetrated her hard. "Oh, oh, yes, yes

I come, so fast my love, fuck me hard as you can, I come again." He could not hold back; he held her tight as he spurted in her. He held her hard until he slipped out.

"Maria, my wonderful, darling Maria, you drive me wild, I just have to see you, smell you, touch you, hear you and I want to fuck you. You are the most irresistible woman in the world."

She smiled seductively, "I know my love, I cannot help talking when you fuck me and I know it turns you on."

"Like nothing else on earth."

She said, "Now we have Champagne and get ready." He dressed in smart casuals, beige chino pants, blue shirt with a button-down collar, cream coloured corduroy jacket, blue socks and brown slip-on shoes, then he watched her dress, a black thong, black uplift bra which just covered her nipples, black slim line skirt which just touched her knees, white short sleeved blouse with a red bow, a short red waist length bolero type jacket, no stockings, her shapely tanned legs set off by high heeled strapless shoes. Her hair in a ponytail tied with a large matching red bow. He just stared and remarked, "You look simply sensational."

She smiled, "You make me feel sensational." They had more Champagne and sat holding hands. He said, "For the first time, I can ever recall, my stomach is like jelly, shaking, I am meeting my mother for the first time, 43 years it has taken to get here."

"Darling, she will be feeling the same as you and wondering what your reaction will be."

At precisely on time, Alex came for them. "Your audience awaits you in one of the conference rooms, they are all excited, a bit tense but dying to see you." He led them, they took the elevator to the second floor. Alex opened the door and ushered them in. When John entered, they were startled by his looks due to the strong resemblance to his father. He was focused on one person; he was oblivious to all the others as he strode forward to Fiona. The tears started to flow, all in the room had risen to their feet. Fiona stood arms outstretched, they grasped each other tight, he said, "Mother, I have dreamt of this moment but thought it would never be. I have been searching for you."

Fiona replied, "Me too, my son, I have looked for you ever since you were taken away."

Tears trickled down their cheeks as they held each other for several minutes, he said, "Mother, this is Maria, we are getting wed in two weeks' time."

The women hugged each other, "My dear, you are beautiful, Adam is a very lucky man."

"I am so lucky too."

Fiona said, "I named you after your father, your name is Adam McEwen, I hope you like it."

"Finally I have my real name, I have used so many in the past. I am proud to have his name."

"You are his double except for your hair."

"Oh that, I dyed it for a specific reason, I will tell you about it sometime, my hair is actually very dark like my father's."

"Come, let me introduce you both to everyone, they can't wait to meet you."

Big hugs from everyone, men and women, as they were introduced, they chatted to everyone, Fiona's father was very emotional, in fact, everyone was, not a dry eye in the house, when they met his paternal grandfather, the Earl of Berwick said, "My boy, you gave me a bit of a shock, I thought it was a ghost walking into the room, your father and you are like twins. This is a wonderful day for all of us." The hours passed, Alex announced, dinner will be served next door in 30 minutes. Adam sat, Fiona on his left, Maria on his right. Dinner was superb, multiple choices for starters, main course, dessert plus cheeses and biscuits. A different wine for each course, Irish coffees and brandy to finish with.

Alex stood up and told them about the plans to establish a special school and it would be very likely sited in Scotland, that Adam and he were the principals, "So, no doubt all of you will see a lot of Maria and Alex in the future, I am certain that Adam wishes to make an announcement, a few of you know what it is already, Adam please tell them."

Adam stood and told them about the wedding, what the preparations were, "You are all invited as our guests, Maria and I dearly desire your presence, however, if any of you are unable to attend, Maria and I will have a second ceremony in Scotland. I hope my mother will assist in organising the ceremony and the reception." He looked at Fiona and Maria, both faces showing their pleasure as he said, "That's definitely a starter." As he sat everyone applauded. Fiona murmured, "That is wonderful." The party went on for some time, the guests began to drift off but bade their goodnights' to Maria and Adam, kissing and hugging them. Everyone was staying at the hotel. Quite a few had a fair few drinks and were hanging on to each other as they slowly ambled off to their rooms. Alex, Maria and Adam were the last to leave. Alex remarked, "The two of you have brought much happiness, I'm off to bed, a most ecstatic old man and a very tired one, goodnight." He left, with an unsteady gait.

"Well, my lovely, darling, sexy girl, are you tired?"

She eyed him with a sexy look, tongue licking her lips suggestively, "No and you're not tired either."

"You are right, the adrenaline is still buzzing, what do you say, we can test the strength of that large bed."

"You know my answer, we have all night so I want you to undress me slowly and I want to feel your lips all over me."
"My God, you know how to drive me crazy, let's go."

They hastened to their room; he complied with her wish, taking his time removing every garment, kissing, licking and touching her all over her body including the most intimate places. She posed in different positions, standing legs apart, lying on her back. Legs apart and high, on her knees as he licked and nibbled her, her body was quivering and convulsing as she climaxed time after time. She placed her hand over her mouth to muffle her screams, she never stopped talking, driving him to greater efforts and variations. As she lay panting and gasping, body heaving, she said, "Now it's your turn, I want to kiss every part of your body, I want to see you come, I will drive you crazy, after, we fuck when you get hard."

She set to work, positioning him, standing, lying on his back as her lips, tongue and fingers touched, licked, nibbled and sucked him. She held him as his body tensed and he spurted as she knelt in front of him, his ejaculations striking her breasts. He knelt down and they embraced. "I did not think it could possibly get better making love with you but that was the most fantastic experience ever."

She stroked him, "My wonderful sexy man, that is the first time I have tried doing these things, what you did was exciting, I loved your lips and tongue inside me, it sent me wild, I could not stop coming, I did not want to stop, I just wanted more and more to feel you inside me. Did you like doing it to me?"

"I loved it, I love watching you come, when your eyes are wide open, your mouth open and panting and your body shaking, it really turns me on and what you did to me was out of this world. I think what you drank tonight removed any inhibitions you had. Anyway, sex between husband and wife should be uninhibited, as long as both enjoy it."

"Adam, I loved it, we will do it lots of times."

"On our wedding night and after, most times I will come inside you but I enjoy you playing with my cock, so we will have a lot of fun at times."

"You are getting hard my love, time to fuck me." She got up and went to a dressing table, she faced the mirror hands on the table, bent forward, "I want to watch you fuck me, I want to see your face when you come deep inside me."

Her words and her position set him aflame, he positioned himself behind her as she reached for him and pushed it in her. They watched each other as he plunged deep inside her, grasping her tight as he rammed her. Her breasts swinging, her mouth open and gasping, eyes open, "Yes, yes, my darling, oh, oh I see stars, I feel dizzy, don't stop, I come many times, fuck me hard," she yelled as he shot into her, holding her hips and bottom tight as he emptied himself. He lay over her back, both panting.

He pulled her up straight, held her tight, "Darling, we better shower, if we go to bed now, we will get stuck to the sheets, both of us are really sticky."

She started to giggle, "Okay, my darling, you are the boss, anything you say." They showered, towelled each other dry and went to bed. Maria fell asleep within minutes, he lay awake, so many thoughts in his mind the adrenaline still coursing through his veins. Eventually, he fell asleep.

The Tenth Day

They did not wake up until after 9 a.m. Both were hungry so a quick shower, quickly dressing and down for breakfast. They entered the dining room, spotted Alex, Fiona and Will sitting at a table so they joined them. Maria and John kissed Fiona's cheeks. Fiona smiled, "Did you have a good night's rest?" She said.

Maria answered with a straight face, "Yes, it was one of the best I have ever had." John dare not reply but looked at Maria whose eyes were twinkling.

Fiona said, "What are your plans for today?"

"I want to go shopping; I am sure Maria wants to visit the shops as well. I want to buy the full highland regalia of the McEwen tartan, the whole outfit, the dress version, I want to wear it at both ceremonies."

"Adam, your grandfather will be so happy, I think that is wonderful." Maria added, "I love it, I want to buy a sash of the same tartan, I have seen pictures in magazines, of girls wearing white and the sash from one shoulder to the waist. It adds colour, very lovely."

"Will and I will come with you, we know the best shops, if that is alright with you both?"

Maria chimed in before Adam could say anything, "Yes, that is ideal, we would love your company."

Adam grinned. "Just occasionally I will allow her to wear the pants in the family." They all laughed. Adam and Maria opted for the full Scottish breakfast, orange juice, a fry up of gammon bacon, eggs, Lorne sliced sausage, black pudding, potato scones, fried bread, mushrooms and tomatoes, he had tea, Maria had coffee. They ate with gusto, during the meal, the grandparents entered the room and came over for a chat.

When they finished eating and were having more tea and coffee, Fiona said, "Is it possible for both of you to spend two or three days in Scotland, I know that you are making preparations for the wedding, the reason I ask is that I would like you to stay with us, visit all your grandparents and have a good look around the estates and countryside, Maria, it's a bit chilly now, so I will get you fitted out with fleeces and sweaters, warm trousers, woollen socks and good walking shoes."

Maria replied, "Yes, we will stay, Mama and Papa are organising the wedding, we would love to see everyone in their homes."

Adam lifted the tablecloth and peered underneath it, he muttered, "I could have sworn that you were wearing a skirt, when did you change?"

Everyone hooted, Maria laughed, "I'll let you make the next decision, you can be boss anywhere except in the kitchen and the bedroom."

"Wow, I'll go for that." Maria flushed slightly and stuck her tongue out at him. He just grinned.

They spent several hours shopping, had a pub lunch at an old public house in the Royal Mile, visited the castle, on their return to the hotel. Packed their belongings and left, the three of them, including Alex being driven in Fiona's and Will's Range Rover. The journey took about three hours which included a stop for afternoon tea and toilet visits. Darkness had long fallen by the time they reached Montrose House. The small team of household staff had been informed and were waiting to greet them. Maria and Adam were introduced to everyone, they included a housekeeper, cook, chambermaid and servant girl. Maria and Adam impressed them with charm and polite respect, winning their affection instantly.

The house was magnificent, centrally heated throughout but with huge open fireplaces in the lounge and bedrooms. A meal had been prepared; the dining room was dominated by a long table that could seat 16 persons.

The meal was game soup, braised venison steaks with a redcurrant sauce and vegetables, rhubarb tart, red wine, coffee and brandy to finish with. Maria commented on the splendid meal, Will said, "We can live off the wildlife, you will see herds of deer, flocks of partridges, pheasants and ducks by the lake, salmon and trout from the river, we have a walled vegetable garden and orchards of apples, pears, plums and damsons. Sarah, the cook makes jams and jellies, preserves fruit in jars. Fiona's father sends us the finest steaks and sides of beef. We hardly ever eat frozen products. Both your grandparents eat the same as us." Alex said, "You won't find finer food anywhere in the world."

After the meal, the five of them went to the library and sat by the blazing fire. Maria remarked what a beautiful home it was, Fiona said, "It is modest compared to the others, they are all spectacular, Alex's house has a beautiful stretch of river running through the estate and the scenery is wonderful, Alex is staying the night, tomorrow we will take him home and you can see what I mean. A grandfather clock chimed 11 o'clock, Adam said, "I am still somewhere in the clouds, it is all a marvellous dream, I'm for bed now, what time do we set off tomorrow?"

Fiona answered, "Not early, sleep in late if you want, cook will get you breakfast, come I'll show your rooms."

She led the way to the first floor, paused outside a door and said with a smile, "I assume you are sharing? A fire has been set in this room but I can set another fire in another room if you wish separate rooms," she said with a twinkle and mischievous smile.

Maria replied with a warm smile, "Thank you, we do sleep together, it's not a secret, we are lovers soon to be wed, neither of us wishes to sleep alone."

"Good for you, you are an honest wonderful woman, the two of you are perfectly matched, have a lovely night."

Adam kissed her as soon as Fiona had left. "You are some lady, my darling, straight and to the point."

She kissed him and looked at the blazing fire, she said, "I have seen movies where there is love making on a shaggy rug in front of a fire, now we will do the same but for real, undress me slowly my darling, I want to feel your tongue, lips and fingers all over my body, my body is burning for you." He obeyed, taking his time making her shudder with her climaxes. "My darling I have come many times, I cannot stop, I am so wet, my love I will do the same to you."

He stood as she took her time undressing him, kissing and nipping him with her teeth, "You are so hard, my love, I love to hold your cock."

Adam was rampant, "Get on your knees in front of the fire now."

She did so as he knelt behind her and thrust into her making her gasp, "I love your hard cock, fuck me hard my love, I am warm and wet for you." As usual, her words inflamed him, he pulled her up slightly holding her breasts, pinching the nipples. "Yes, yes, I like that, I love everything you do to me, darling, I keep coming, oh, oh I cannot stop, I am so wet."

"My darling I am going to come any second." She pulled forward, turned round to face him and took hold of him and masturbated him aiming his cock at her breasts, he spurted several times, the globules of sperm splattering her breasts, she kept milking him until the last drop, "My darling, I love watching you come, it excites me, I always come when you fire your sperm onto me. Do you like it?"

"I love it when you hold my cock I want to cover you with my come. I can't get enough of you; you are so sexy." She then surprised him by saying, "We do 69 now?"

He said, "Where did you hear that, do you know what it is?"

She smiled sexily, "I read it in a magazine, many women write letters saying it is very good."

"Good grief is nothing sacred in magazines these days, you do know what it is?"

"Yes, it is giving each other oral love at the same time, I want to do it, do you want to do it?"

"Of course, it is very popular, I think most lovers do it and many who are not lovers do it too." She stroked him until he grew firm, "My love, you are hard, I lie down with you on top and then we change places, you lie down and I will be on top."

The session continued until both were spent, they lay side by side, bodies heaving. "Maria, my love I am well and truly knackered, that was a marathon, it was out of this world. I loved every moment." She raised herself leaning on one arm and gazed at him with dilated sex-laden eyes, "I loved it, I love everything we do, I love your lips on me, I love it when you lick me, when you taste me. I loved your cock in my mouth, I love tasting you, I love when you come in my mouth. Did you like coming in my mouth?"

"Yes, very much, my love everything we do just shows how much we love each other, everything we do is sensational and your talking is a massive turn on, I get hard when you start talking then I just want to fuck you."

"Good, I never stop talking when we make love, I want you hard all the time."

"Maria, love, we better shower, we are covered in sticky come."

"I like feeling your sticky body against mine but we shower and go to bed." By the time they showered and got snuggled up in bed, they were so weary, they fell asleep in no time.

Visits

The next two days were spent visiting, seeing Alex's house and estate then visits to both sets of grandparents. Maria and Adam were surprised by the magnificent houses, grounds and size of the estates. They met all the employees, spoke to them, all were very happy at their work and well paid with excellent insurance schemes, many in tied accommodation such as large cottages guaranteed that when they retired they could remain paying a very small rental. Adam learnt much about running the estates. Three days later they left to return to Spain, as the plane gained height after take-off, Adam grasped Maria's hand and thought of the future. He mused, how fortunate could a person be, he was with the most wonderful, beautiful woman; he had a brilliant job, heir to several estates, he would inherit several titles he was now a Viscount, there would also be many challenges ahead but with Maria by his side, he had no doubt that all would be overcome.

Epilogue

The wedding in Malaga was a magical event for Maria and Adam, it was well organised and attended by all the Scottish members of his family, between them they hired a private jet to avoid all the rigmarole of queuing at the airport. Adam and Alex wore the McEwen highland dress tartan. Maria looked spectacular in a white full length dress with a train, her headdress was a tiara and veil, she wore the McEwen tartan sash. Their wedding night was spent in a Malaga hotel. The following day they jetted out, destination, the Seychelles for two weeks.

They returned to Spain for a few days and then went to Scotland, staying with Fiona and Will whilst looking for a suitable residence and grounds to establish the school.

Alex assisted. They did find a very suitable establishment that met many of their requirements.

It was a very large castle sited in Perthshire, until recently it had been a boys military academy, it originally had 180 rooms but many had been altered to form dormitories, it would be renovated to its former state. There were a number of outbuildings used as classrooms. A separate 4 bedroom, two storied house which was located in the grounds overlooking a loch had been the residence of the principal, it required decorating and renovating the kitchen and bathrooms, two of the bedrooms had en suite facilities.

There was a large covered heated swimming pool situated near the classrooms. There was an outdoor firing range. Set in magnificent scenery and 7 miles from the nearest village, there was a gatehouse and then a mile long tarmac drive to the castle. The grounds had an abundance of different deciduous trees and a few evergreens. Deer and red squirrels could be seen on the estate. Adam, Maria and Alex all loved it.

It was another 8 months before the initial course started, instructors/teachers had been appointed. Wolf (Brian Cook) had been appointed administrator/office manager.

The first course consisted of 18 students, minimum age 24 years, maximum age 35 years, Only 3 failed the course.

Ten months after the wedding, Maria gave birth to a daughter, christened Fiona, Rosita McEwen, 18 months after that, a son was born christened Adam, Ramon.

Maria and Adam were in heaven. Both births took place in Scotland.

It was 4 years before the ranch was bought, situated midway between Malaga and Granada. It was a huge sprawling place, dominated by the main house and had several smaller residences, all detached, modernised, stables for 20 horses, two large corrals for breaking in and training them. Two streams ran through the estate, in the Summer months they were very dry but there was a large reservoir and the ranch had wells. The land was uncultivated except for a large olive grove, many shrubs and trees dotted the landscape.

Adam's commission and rewards for the recovery of all the items came to over 15 million pounds and his salary met all the wages and expenses of the ranch. Diego resigned and was the ranch manager/overseer, his family were housed next to the main house.

For all concerned life could not be better.